The Legend of the Bells and Other Tales

The Legend of the Bells and Other Tales

Stories of the Human Spirit

John Shea

ACTA
ASSISTING CHRISTIANS TO ACT
PUBLICATIONS

The Legend of the Bells and Other Tales: Stories of the Human Spirit by John Shea

Edited by Gregory F. Augustine Pierce
Cover Design and Art by Tom A. Wright
Typesetting by Garrison Publications

ISBN: 087946-147-0   Library of Congress Catalog Number: 96-85729

Printed in the United States of America

01 00 99 97 96 5 4 3 2 1 First Printing

Table of Contents

To the stories my father told

and

the story my father is.

Introduction

The stories in this book are not chicken soup for the soul. They may console you, but their mission is not consolation. They may inspire you, but their aim is not inspiration. They may soothe you out of sickness, but they do not pride themselves on being soothing. If they do these things, it is not because they have ministered to an ailing soul that needs to be consoled, inspired and healed. The reason lies elsewhere.

The truth is that the soul does not need chicken soup. Nor does the soul need to be cared for. There is nothing wrong with the soul. Jack Canfield has it right:

> Let me begin by saying that I think there is a big difference between "nourishing your soul" and "being nourished by your soul." We don't

nourish our soul. Our soul nourishes us. We don't do something to our soul so much as have our soul do something for us. Our challenge as human beings is to open ourselves to receive this nourishment—to rekindle our connection with our spirit, the spirit that is always there waiting to nurture, heal, and direct our lives.

If we feel consoled, inspired and healed by these stories, it is because they have connected us with the loving vitality of soul. And soul is doing what soul always does when it is not blocked: It is pouring spirit that it has received from the divine source into our troubled minds, our tumultuous emotions, our racked bodies, our tortured relationships, our fragmented society, our wounded earth.

Of course, most of us are not in touch with soul. We do not know how to rest in the soul space and see and act out of that space. As the Christian mystical tradition has continuously asserted, the soul has two eyes—one peers into the eternal and one peers into the temporal. When these two eyes are held open, we bring together spirit and flesh, God and world. However, we are often "soul blind," unable to see with both these eyes. We cannot keep consciousness in the soul space. It drifts and splinters, chasing after every stray thought, attracted by every shiny surface. We must learn to pull consciousness back to its source, to lead it home, to allow it to coincide with soul.

This is the service that stories of the human spirit render. They work with our awareness until we are once again seeing from the viewpoint of the soul.

This service does not happen in only one way but through a whole array of strategies and techniques. Some stories delight in lampooning conventional ideas. They think that if they can break the hold these ideas have on our minds, we will be open to deeper levels of perception. Some stories work at reimaging our relationship to God. They hope the new images will facilitate the flow of the spirit. Some stories describe characters who see with the eyes of the soul, and we are slowly and subtly asked to peer through their eyes. Some stories show us characters unable to see with the eyes of the soul in situations where soul-sight is essential. We watch them stumble and fall and thus preview the pitfalls that await us. Stories with these kinds of spiritual ambitions use many tricks, all aimed at drawing our awareness into the grace and life of the soul.

What types of stories are these?

Any type. I am not a story purist. I love all kinds of stories. I tell stories from my own experiences and stories other people have told me about their experiences. I use sections of novels and short stories. I rummage through collections of stories from religious traditions—Sufi, Hindu, Buddhist, Muslim, Jewish, Christian, etc. I find stories tucked away in books of theology and spirituality. I listen to folktales and fairy tales. When the muse visits, I write stories I think will help turn the mind toward the light. The only criterion in my using a story is this: Does it have the potential to bring consciousness into the soul space?

As important as stories are, however, they are not enough. Even if a story works and soul and consciousness coincide, I have always felt the need to talk about it further. I like to try to describe in non-story language what I found in a story. This analysis is not meant to replace the story. To my mind, such reflection complements a story and makes explicit the truths it suggested to me.

Any one reflection, of course, does not exhaust the wisdom a story has to offer. It is only what one teller has discovered, the witness of a single receiver. Reflective language never claims any definitive authority over a story. For me it is just the natural thing to do when a story works. Story language and reflective language are two moments in the single process of the expression and communication of spiritual truth.

This book is a series of stories and reflections. My hope is that each one in particular and all of them together will invade the structures of your awareness and bring you into the space that awaits your homecoming...your soul.

The Antique Watch

For twenty years, I was a teacher. At Christmas-time, it was the custom at the school where I taught for all the kids to bring gifts.

After about the third year, I could name the gift by the size of the box it came in. Whenever my students would come up with long, flat boxes, I would know they were handkerchiefs. Since thank-you notes were not expected, I would take these long, flat boxes and just throw them in my closet unopened. Then, as I needed a handkerchief, I would open a box and take one out. I always had more boxes than I needed handkerchiefs.

One time I went into my closet, took out a box, and opened it. Instead of a handkerchief, there was an antique pocket watch. All this time, I possessed an antique pocket watch and I didn't know it.

"I possessed an antique pocket watch and didn't know it." So thought the school teacher who told me this story.

We own a vintage wine cellar, but we never drink from it. So thought Meister Eckhart.

We have an inner fountain that springs up into eternal life, but we are so out of touch with it we look only in outer wells for water. So thought Jesus.

All of these images suggest that we humans are something very valuable, but we are not in touch with the treasure that we are and the riches that are already ours.

The question naturally arises: Why do we not know who we are and what we have?

Spiritual teachers, who seldom answer questions straight on, think the problem is rooted in the fact that we are multidimensional beings. The human person is comprised of physical, psychological, social and spiritual dimensions. While these dimensions are ultimately integrated into the single reality of who we are, we do not always appreciate these dimensions equally.

If we have a full head of hair, for example, we tend to confer on it a "This is me" quality and designate ourselves as "He of the radiant locks." If we manage an A in economics, we quickly collapse ourselves into this academic glory and become "She of the great intellect." If we work as a Chief Operating Officer in a marketing firm, we may find our attachment to this position so complete that we say to ourselves and others (as if nothing more could be said), "I am a COO." If we have had a powerful experience of being abandoned by someone we love, we may so internalize that single, transitory experience that we think of ourselves forevermore as "The rejected one." Or if we are successful at ingratiating ourselves with other people, we may come to know ourselves as "The charmer."

At any given moment we are tempted to equate our identity with a physical quality, a mental attribute, a social role, a significant experience, or a personality trait. In this sense, our identity is always shifting, attracted to the "bright and shining" flux of our physical, psychological and social dimensions.

However, there is another aspect to human reality, an aspect that often goes unnoticed, a dimension that can remain hidden—like an antique watch in a handkerchief box.

We are also a spiritual reality. At our deepest selves, we are sons and daughters of the Most High. In Jesus' images we are the light of the world, the salt of the earth, a blessedness that defies every negative situation from mourning to persecution.

This spiritual dimension of our being is very subtle, however. Allowing our consciousness to coincide with it is very difficult. So we usually do not even recognize that it is there. We constantly make the mistake of identifying ourselves with our body, mind or social position. But the fullness of who we are is *always a little bit more than any of that.*

St. Paul said we hold a treasure in earthen vessels. But we are more aware of the earthen vessel than the treasure, I think. We also have an antique pocket watch in a hand-kerchief box. But we are more aware of the handkerchief box than the antique watch, I think.

Both Here
and
There

It seems that in ancient times there was a king named Akbar, who had a brilliant and clever prime minister named Birbal. Akbar was always asking questions that he hoped would baffle Birbal, but Birbal was always able to answer and so save his life and his ministership.

One day Akbar asked Birbal if he could bring him someone who was Here and not There. Birbal brought him a thief, saying, "This thief is only in the world trying to get money and goods to increase his wealth Here."

Then Akbar told Birbal, "Bring me someone who is There and not Here." Birbal responded by bringing a wandering ascetic—a *sadhu* or mendicant—and said, "He completely neglects all aspects of this world, including his body and his well-being, to focus entirely on the world beyond."

"Very good," said Akbar. "Now bring me someone who is neither Here nor There." Birbal left for a while and then returned, presenting to the king a beggar, saying, "This man is neither Here nor There, because he is always envious of everyone else in the world. He's not participating in the world in any sense and, at the same time, has no concern for spiritual matters. Thus, he is in no way There either."

"Very good again," exclaimed a pleased Akbar. "Now, is it possible that there is anyone in the world who is both Here and There?"

"Yes, your majesty," answered Birbal, and he brought forth an honest householder couple. "This man and woman work in the world and tend to their family, but do everything with God in their thoughts. Because they do the work of the world and allow their spiritual practices to carry them through both the good and the bad times, they are a man and woman who are both Here and There."

"Very good," said Akbar, and immediately began to think about the next challenge he would give Birbal.

"Master," said the disciple, "I saw a man who could fly."

"So?" said the master, "a bird can fly."

"Master," said the disciple, "I saw a man who could live under water."

"So?" said the master, "a fish can live under water."

"Master," said the disciple, "I saw a man who could, in the twinkling of an eye, move from one town to another."

"So?" said the master, "Satan can do that."

"If you wish to find something truly extraordinary," the master explained, "find a man who can be among people and keep his thoughts on God."

This little master-disciple exchange has the same point as Birbal's final cleverness. The trick is to be both here and there. People can be this-worldly (here but not there) or otherworldly (there but not here) or neither (not here and not there). But the spiritual ideal is dual consciousness. Meister Eckhart described dual consciousness as a hinge and a door. The hinge stayed perfectly still while the door swung to and fro, letting in and letting out the many things of the world. This ideal is also expressed in the phrase "in the world, but not of the world."

In Luke's famous story, Martha and Mary are often interpreted in this way. Martha and Mary are sisters. Therefore, they are two sides of a single dynamic. They are not meant to be contrasted but rather integrated into the Christian ideal of contemplation in action. In this interpretation, the problem is not that Martha is acting but that she is acting in a worried, resentful and anxious way. Her actions are scattered and therefore ineffective. She wants to pull Mary out of the peaceful space she is in and into the frantic world Martha is inhabiting at the moment. However, what is really needed ("Only one thing is needed") is for Martha to make the same spiritual step as Mary. Jesus never suggested that either of them leave the world of activity. They need to be both here and there at the same time.

What can be said about this spiritual ideal of contemplation in action?

Well, sometimes it seems to just happen and, there is no denying it, it is a mellow space to be in. But most of the time we manage "both here and there" only as a tourist. We are soon back and buried in "here" or drifting off into "there." Achieving "both here and there" is easier said than done, and easier done once in a while than on a regular basis.

The Christmas
Phone Call

"Ma, come to the table," Ellen said in a voice that betrayed nothing.

It was Christmas afternoon. The five Dolans—Tom and Ellen, their children Marge, Patrick and Catlin—and Ellen's mother, Marie McKenzie, had gone to church, opened presents, and lingered forever over a Christmas drink. Dinner was now on the table.

Marie said she was not hungry. She rocked back and forth in her favorite chair. On the table next to her was the phone.

"Ma, if she is going to call, she will call. Come to the table."

Marie just rocked.

Ellen gestured her husband Tom into the kitchen. "I spend all day on this meal and she is letting it get cold. This is the thanks I get. All year I take care of her. Take her to bingo, the hair dresser's, church. And every holiday she sulks there waiting for that daughter of hers to call."

Tom had heard all this before. "I don't think she's sulking," said Tom. "I'll take care of it."

Tom went back into the living room, right past Marie at her telephone post, and up the stairs to their bedroom. Marie pretended she didn't see him.

Tom took their phone listings out of the dresser drawer and dialed the California number.

"Yeah!" said a groggy man's voice.

Oh no, thought Tom, not another one. "Is Ann there?"

"Minute."

"Hello."

"Ann, this is Tom. Merry Christmas. Call your mother."

"Tom, for Christ's sake, it's only noon out here, I'll call her later."

"Now, Ann. We can't get her to come to the table and eat. Ellen is doing a slow burn."

"So what's new?" She waited, but Tom said nothing.

"O.K. I'll call."

Tom was halfway down the stairs when the phone rang.

Marie answered it on the second ring.

"Hi ya, Mom. Ellen feeding you enough?"

"Oh Annie, it's so good to hear your voice."

"Good to hear yours too, Mom. I went to midnight Mass and was sleeping late." She reached under the covers and gave Hank a squeeze. He didn't move. He had fallen back to sleep.

"By the way, Mom, I got your check. Thanks. I needed it."

"You're welcome. When will you be in Chicago?"

"Spring sometime. I'll let you know."

"I miss you."

"You've got Ellen right there, Mom." Her voice got louder as if her mother were hard of hearing.

"Would you like to talk to her?"

There was a moment of silence. "Why not?"

"Here she is."

Ellen had been listening to each word from the kitchen doorway. She walked toward her mother, wiping her hands on her apron. Marie held out the phone. The cord was stretched to the full.

Ellen took the phone. "Merry Christmas."

"Merry Christmas," returned Ann.

Ellen gave the phone back to her mother.

"There," Marie said to anyone who was listening. Her voice had a sense of accomplishment as if she had just carried a great weight up a forbidding hill and set it down right where it should be. "Merry Christmas," she said out loud to herself.

Then Marie puckered a kiss into the phone's receiver and said, "Bye, Annie, don't let the bedbugs bite."

"Oh, Mom," Ann managed before her mother hung up.

Marie came immediately to the table. The children were stifling laughs; Tom was smiling; Ellen was staring at the plate.

They recited grace together. The food was passed and piled high on each plate.

Marie poured the tea into her cup, poured the tea from the cup onto her saucer, then blew on it to cool it off. A forkful of dressing went into her mouth.

"Delicious," she said with her mouth full.

"Oh, Mom," sighed Ellen.

Act One

I wrote this story because of the not-too-subtle suggestion of an irritated woman: "I always hear about the prodigal son but not the prodigal daughter."

I answered, "Well, the story is really more about the father than the younger son. It is a tale about the father's response to both sons in their different estrangements and how he is trying to bring them back into relationship with one another."

"Same difference, don't you think?" And she walked away.

Her problem with the story was the lack of female presence.

Act Two

At a party between Christmas and New Year's, I innocently asked a woman, "How was your Christmas?"

"Terrible. My mother wouldn't come to the table before my nitwit sister called from California. Finally, I got my husband to call California and tell her to call Mom."

"Thank you," I said. "You've given me the idea I need."

"What do you mean?"

I explained.

Act Three

If there is any line at all between single-mindedness and outright stubbornness, it is a thin one. Marie will not come to the feast until her daughters have talked to each other. Christmas without at least a gesture of reconciliation is foreign to her. No matter what else is happening, the one thing the mother has to have is renewed dialogue between her daughters. Until that happens, the outpost by the phone will be womaned.

Just as in the gospel story, there is tremendous resistance on the part of both daughters, and the resistance is by no means broken down. However, in this story a momentary and involuntary truce happens. The two sisters exchange the greetings of the season, "Merry Christmas." We do not know if a second baby step down the road of reconciliation will ever be taken. Of course, in the

Lukan original we do not know if the older son ever goes into the feast. Both stories focus first on the passion of the reconcilers and then on the movement or lack of movement in the resistant parties. The mother (as presumably the Prodigal Father did) is eating with gusto. Her older daughter is left with the option of joining her or nurturing a resentment that does not aid digestion. Her response to this hang-tough mama of togetherness is a frustrated recognition of her true nature, "Oh, Mom!" Mother is one who gives life even when it is not requested or even (sometimes) accepted.

Act Four

Over the years I have gotten goofy on the subject of reconciliation. I know less and less about how it happens. I have no confidence in trying to map it out step-by-step. All I am sure of is that when it does happen, it is usually serendipitous, unexpected and a surprise to all.

However, as I have become less certain about how it happens, I have become more convinced that it will happen. I have been there when people say, "Never!" I have said, "Never!" But in the back of my mind there is an uninvited voice that is always saying, "Someday." Maybe it is our Divinely Prodigal Mother/Father speaking.

Someone once described love as the power that drives everything there is toward everything else that is. This love permeates the universe, holding it together. Divine glue. In order to stay apart we actually have to resist this pull toward communion. This resistance takes considerable energy and inventiveness. Of course, we are always up to the task. Never underestimate human persistence in estrangement! We can and do refuse the everlasting offer to come together. However, I am betting that we will eventually weaken. The rumor on the streets is that the Holy Spirit melts hearts. Global warming may or may not be an atmospheric fact, but in the world of spirit it is an ever-present possibility. Thawing the frozen is what the Holy Spirit does for a living.

People say this confidence in eventual reconciliation is the product of a well-developed sense of fantasy. They point out all the cases where it doesn't happen. They ask, "What about death? How can reconciliation occur when one person has died?"

I throw a hand in the air. "Since when is death a barrier?"

As I said, I've gotten a little goofy on reconciliation.

The Fasting of the Heart

Yen Hui, the favorite disciple of Confucius, came to take leave of his Master.

"Where are you going?" asked Confucius.

"I am going to Wei."

"And for what?"

"I have heard that the Prince of Wei is a lusty full-blooded fellow and is entirely self-willed. He takes no care of his people and refuses to see any fault in himself. He pays no attention to the fact that his subjects are dying right and left. Corpses lie all over the country like hay in a field. The people are desperate. But I have heard you, Master, say that one should leave the state that is well-governed and go to that which is in disorder. At the door of the physician there are plenty of sick people. I want to take this opportunity to put into practice what I have learned from you and see if I can bring about some improvement in conditions there."

"Alas!" said Confucius, "you do not realize what you are doing. You will bring disaster upon yourself. Tao has no need of your eagerness, and you will only waste your energy in your misguided efforts. Wasting your energy you will become confused and then anxious. Once anxious, you will no longer be able to help yourself. The sages of old first sought Tao in themselves, then looked to see if there was anything in others that corresponded with Tao as they knew it. But if you do not have Tao yourself, what business have you spending your time in vain efforts to bring corrupt politicians into the right path?...However, I suppose you must have some basis for your hope of success. How do you propose to go about it?"

Yen Hui replied: "I intend to present myself as a humble, disinterested man, seeking only to do what is right and nothing else: a completely simple and honest approach. Will this win his confidence?"

"Certainly not," Confucius replied. "This man is convinced that he alone is right. He may pretend outwardly to take an interest in an objective standard of justice, but do not be deceived by his expression. He is not accustomed to being opposed by anyone. His way is to reassure himself that he is right by trampling on other people. If he does this with mediocre men, he will all the more certainly do it to one who presents a threat by claiming to be a man of high qualities. He will cling stubbornly to his own way. He may pretend to be interested in your talk about what is objectively right, but interiorly he will not hear you, and there will be no change whatever. You will get nowhere with this."

Yen Hui then said: "Very well. Instead of directly opposing him, I will maintain my own standards interiorly, but outwardly I will appear to yield. I will appeal to the authority of traditions and to the examples of the past. He who is interiorly uncompromising is a son of heaven just as much as any ruler. I will not rely on any teaching of my own, and will consequently have no concern about whether I am approved or not. I will eventually be recognized as perfectly disinterested and sincere. They will all come to appreciate my candor, and thus I will be an instrument of heaven in their midst.

"In this way, yielding in obedience to the Prince as other men do, bowing, kneeling, prostrating myself as a servant should, I shall be accepted without blame. Then others will have confidence in me, and gradually they will make use of me, seeing that I desire only to make myself useful and to work for the good of all. Thus I will be an instrument of men.

"Meanwhile, all I have to say will be expressed in terms of ancient tradition. I will be working with the sacred tradition of the ancient sages. Though what I say may be objectively a condemnation of the Prince's conduct, it will not be I who say it, but tradition itself. In this way, I will be perfectly honest, and yet not give offense. Thus I will be an instrument of tradition. Do you think I have the right approach?"

"Certainly not," said Confucius. "You have too many different plans of action, when you have not even got to know the Prince and observed his character! At best, you might get away with it and save your skin, but you will not change anything whatever. He might perhaps superficially conform to your words, but there will be no real change of heart."

Yen Hui then said: "Well, that is the best I have to offer. Will you, Master, tell me what you suggest?"

"You must fast!" said Confucious. "Do you know what I mean by fasting? It is not easy. But easy ways do not come from God."

"Oh," said Yen Hui, "I am used to fasting! At home we were poor. We went for months without wine or meat. That is fasting, is it not?"

"Well, you can call it 'observing a fast' if you like," said Confucius, "but it is not the fasting of the heart."

"Tell me," said Yen Hui, "what is fasting of the heart?"

Confucius replied: "The goal of fasting is inner unity. This means hearing, but not with the ear; hearing, but not with the understanding; hearing with the spirit, with your whole being. The hearing that is only in the ears is one thing. The hearing of the understanding is another. But the hearing of the spirit is not limited to any one faculty, to the ear, or to the mind. Hence it demands the emptiness of all the faculties. And when the faculties are empty, then the whole being listens. There is then a direct grasp of what is right there before you that can never be heard with the ear or understood with the mind. Fasting of the heart empties the faculties, frees you from limitation and from preoccupation. Fasting of the heart begets unity and freedom."

"I see," said Yen Hui. "What was standing in my way was my own self-awareness. If I can begin this fasting of the heart, self-awareness will vanish. Then I will be free from limitation and preoccupation! Is that what you mean?"

"Yes," said Confucius, "that's it! If you can do this, you will be able to go among men in their world without upsetting them. You will not enter into conflict with their ideal image of themselves. If they will listen, sing them a song. If not, keep silent. Don't try to break down their door. Don't try out new medicines on them. Just be there among them, because there is nothing else for you to be but one of them. Then you may have success!

"It is easy to stand still and leave no trace, but it is hard to walk without touching the ground. If you follow human methods, you can get away with deception. In the way of Tao, no deception is possible.

"You know that one can fly with wings; you have not yet learned about flying without wings. You are familiar with the wisdom of those who know, but you have not yet learned the wisdom of those who know not.

"Look at this window; it is nothing but a hole in the

wall, but because of it the whole room is full of light. So when the faculties are empty, the heart is full of light. Being full of light it becomes an influence by which others are secretly transformed."

"The sages of old first sought Tao in themselves, then looked to see if there was anything in others that corresponded with Tao as they knew it."

Tao is difficult to paraphrase. Literally it means "the way." By extension it means a universal presence in all things that is ceaselessly working for harmony. If we are in touch with Tao in ourselves, we will recognize it at work in the situations we seek to improve. This piece of spiritual advice seems sound, but we seldom go about things in sound ways.

Instead, when we see a situation that needs

changing, we immediately perform a force field analysis (gauging what factors will help us and what factors will hinder us), make an intervention, and conduct an evaluation. Then we begin the process over again with another analysis, another intervention, and another evaluation. We are problem solvers, absorbed in the fluctuations of the outer world.

Yen Hui, the favorite disciple of Confucius, is one of us. The outside situation is the disorder in the country and the key player is the prince. Yen Hui proposes many strategies on how to approach the prince in order to bring about change. However, all his ploys are based on an analysis of a prince he has never met. His plans also entail playing a role, pretending to be someone he is not. He is willing to analyze endlessly and compromise himself thoroughly—all in the name of social change. He is eager, but as Confucius tells him, "Tao has no need of your eagerness." What he needs to consider is the inner work that is necessary for outer action.

This inner work is the fasting of the heart. When Yen Hui hears the word "fast," he immediately thinks of refraining from food. This is a narrative device that St. John would recognize, since so many of the characters in his gospel make the same mistake. They are stuck on the level of the physical, as is Yen Hui. The Johannine Jesus often attempts to move them to the deeper level of spirit, as Confucius does in "The Fasting of the Heart."

Confucius is talking, rather, about Yen Hui refraining from all ideas and strategies, fasting from the products of his mind. This fast will allow him to see "what is right there before you." Yen Hui finally gets the point. "What was standing in my way was my own self-awareness." This is the first correct thing the favorite disciple says in the story.

Confucius builds on this insight by spelling out the effects of fasting from your own self-awareness. Yen Hui will be able to go among people without entering into conflict with their own idealized self-images. He will not be trying to save them, but just be there with them. Finally, he will become a window that is "nothing but a hole in the wall, but because of it the entire room is filled with light." This light somehow facilitates change in others.

These final paragraphs of the story, these last images and insights of Confucius are provocative and tantalizing. They ring true and I sense they are onto something important. But it is difficult to spell out exactly what Confucius is proposing.

I am reminded of a Sufi teaching of Rais El-Aflak: "Almost all the men who come to see me have strange imaginings about man. The strangest of these is the belief that they can progress only by improvement. Those who understand me are those who realize that man is just as much in need of stripping off rigid accretions to reveal the knowing essence as he is of adding anything."

Could it be that Confucius advises Yen Hui to strip off accretions and that the resulting emptiness becomes the hole through which light will appear? Is it then the nature of this light to allow others to strip off their accretions? Is Tao always there and must we merely detach ourselves from all that is not Tao and it will emerge?

This is quite a gamble for activists who seek change. To work on themselves as the most *effective way to open others to change seems the long way around. It is certainly the diffi-cult way around. Is there a place for Tao in the world of change agents?*

The Fasting Monk

An abbot and a new monk go to the home of a couple and their children to have dinner.

The couple have put out quite a spread, and everyone is eating. But the young monk has vowed that he would fast, and so he takes only a celery stick, which he carves up nicely and eats.

On the way home, the abbot says to him, "The next time, fast from your virtue."

Ah, virtue!

To be good, noble, righteous. To conform to an ideal.

Better yet, to be known as good, to be appreciated as noble, to be rumored as righteous, to be seen as a paragon.

When a tree falls in the forest does it make a sound if no one is there to hear it? If you do something that is good and no one is there to "put it in your permanent record" is it really a virtuous deed?

I once went to the hospital with a woman to see a mutual friend who was sick. When we arrived he was asleep. We waited awhile and then left. In the elevator the woman joked, "We are not going to get any credit for this!"

Goodness often seeks applause. The sound of one hand clapping may be a Buddhist kaon that leads to enlightenment, but the sound of no hands clapping is just frustration to the professionally righteous.

Nothing calls more attention to oneself than fasting at a feast. Look at Marcellus the Monk chewing on celery without salt. What an admirable man!

When goodness becomes an ego project, it secretly cultivates a disdain for others. St. Luke prefaces one of the parables of Jesus with this remark: "This parable was told to those who believed in their own self-righteousness while holding everyone else in contempt." St. Matthew tries to counteract this tendency by recommending "hidden virtue." When you pray, do not stand on street corners. When you give alms, do not blow a trumpet. "When you fast, do not look dismal like the hypocrites, for they disfigure their faces so that their fasting may be seen." The path of true virtue may be to fast from virtue when virtue is part of an overall project of grandiosity.

It seems that virtue should not call attention to itself. The right hand should not know what the left hand is doing. Goodness should be an easy flow of grace, uncalculating and natural.

Of course, if it is, Chuang Tzu points out the terrible results: "In the age when life on earth was full, no one paid any special attention to worthy men, nor did they single out the man of ability. Rulers were simply the highest branches on the trees and the people were like deer in the woods. They were honest and righteous without realizing that they were 'doing their duty.' They loved each other and did not know this was 'love of neighbor.' They deceived no one yet did not know they were 'men to be trusted.' They were reliable and did not know that this was 'good faith.' They lived freely together giving and taking and did not know they were 'generous.' For this reason their deeds have not been narrated. They made no history."

The Father's Bowl

A young girl grew up in a very loving family in a small village. When she woke up in the morning, there were her brothers and sisters, her mother and father. When she worked in the fields during the day, she worked not only with them but with her aunts and uncles and cousins. The entire village was related in one way or another.

At night, when they came together, they all ate in one large hall from common bowls that they passed around to one another. They talked about the history of their people and the relationships that should be and would be among them.

The girl grew up and, in the way of things, she married a man from another village and went to his house to live. The first night she was there, she and her husband sat down around a small table and ate rice from a porcelain bowl. The man's father sat in a corner and ate rice from a wooden bowl.

"My husband," the woman asked, "why do you shame your father? He sits in the corner, eating rice from a wooden bowl."

The husband said to her, "When I was young, he wronged me. He is only receiving what he deserves."

The woman knew, as was the custom of those long-ago days and that far-away place, that she could not ask a second time the reason for any action of her husband.

But the next night, she went to her husband's father as he lay in the corner on his mat, and she said, "To-morrow, break the bowl."

Her father-in-law said, "Woman, if I break the bowl, my son will make me eat rice out of my hands."

She said, "Trust me. Break the bowl."

The next day, after she ladled rice from the pot into the porcelain bowl that she and her husband ate from, she went to the corner to put rice into the wooden bowl of her husband's father, but the bowl was broken.

She turned and said, "My husband, your father has broken the wooden bowl he eats from."

The husband spun around and shouted, "You shouldn't have done that, old man."

The wife said, "You are right, my husband, he should not have broken the bowl. For I was saving that bowl for you, when you grow old and your sons make you eat rice out of it."

This story has a thousand variations and is found in almost every culture. Some renditions do not focus on a past hurt between father and son, but on the simple fact that the father is old and not productive. The son says, "You only take up room and eat." Then the son makes his father climb into a coffin, puts

the coffin in a wheelbarrow, and is about to push it over a cliff. From inside the coffin the father says, "If you were truly frugal, my son, you would take me out of the coffin and just throw me over the cliff. That way your sons will not have to buy a new coffin when it is your turn."

The workings of the story change from rendition to rendition, and so put a different spin on the father-son dynamics. However, the ending remains the same. The son is reminded that what he does to the father will be done to him.

I have told this story and its variations in a number of groups. At the end there is often a collective gasp. I read this gasp as the shock of the obvious. People do not see it coming, yet when it comes its truth is overwhelming and undeniable. For some reason it does not occur to us immediately that what the son is doing to the father will almost certainly be done to him.

I think this blind spot is because we do not understand the inevitability of our evil deeds rebounding back on us. It is just not built into our regular ways of perception. "The measure by which you measure will be measured unto you" is not a gospel lesson that we have learned well.

Down deep, we all harbor some hope that we can get away with our sins. We cannot. We think our evil deeds won't catch up with us. They will. We think no one will know, but we overlook the crucial fact that we know. One of our most persistent illusions is that there are no consequences for ourselves of the wrongs we do. Shedding this illusion can be a major moment in spiritual development.

What we usually stress is how evil deeds affect others. At one time or another everyone has heard the biblical warning, "The parents have eaten sour grapes and the children's teeth are set on edge." In other words, sin is not a private and individual affair. It is passed on from generation to generation, and it has staying power. In another metaphor, unleashed evil "goes about like a roaring lion seeking whom it may devour." We know the contagion of evil and the indiscriminate way it harms and terrorizes. Our horror at sin is generated by the sight of its victims.

"The Father's Bowl" presupposes this general understanding of the spread of evil, but its purpose is to remind us of an often forgotten fact: Evildoers are themselves devoured. They set their own teeth on edge. The son's cruel treatment of his father will someday be visited upon him.

Why does this lesson slip so easily from our sight? Is it that the horror that is inflicted on others occupies us so completely that we cannot focus on the horror that evildoers do to themselves? Is it that we think this is their just punishment for what they have done? Is it that we avoid admitting this truth because we cannot bear to look at our own sin and the way it is killing us?

Perhaps it is just that we do not know how our punishment will happen. Do we believe that God intervenes and makes sure, as Shakespeare wrote, that we are "hoisted on our own petard"? Is there some unconscious psychological accounting that is continually evening the score? To put it in another language, is karma, the consequences of our deeds, so ineluctable that we always get our "karmuppance"?

Whatever our reasons are for avoiding the "truth of consequences," it remains. People never ultimately get off the hook for what they have done precisely because it is they who have put themselves on the hook by doing it. As long as we remain ignorant of this truth, the proverb holds: "Sow the wind, reap the whirlwind."

God's Fruit Stand

A woman went into a marketplace, looked around, and saw a sign that read "God's Fruit Stand."

"Thank goodness. It's about time," the woman said to herself.

She went inside and she said, "I would like a perfect banana, a perfect cantaloupe, a perfect strawberry, and a perfect peach."

God, who was behind the counter, shrugged and said, "I'm sorry. I sell only seeds."

A story is told of William James, the American philosopher-psychologist. At his sixtieth birthday party he announced that he had finally come to believe in life after death. When people asked what had changed his mind, he said, "I am only now becoming fit to live."

When I first read this anecdote, I was struck by the punch line. "I am only now becoming fit to live" is a sentiment that I have often entertained. It usually enters my mind after I have shed some burden and feel more free to say and do things that will be truer to myself and contribute more to other people. Or the phrase enters my mind when I see into reality in a particularly illuminating way and so feel (rightly or wrongly) that I am finally ready to enter the fray as a real player. In fact, sometimes I thank God that I have lived long enough to have "this one" insight and do "this one" thing.

William James pushes this concept even further along. For him, even death is but one more moment in a process of becoming. Could that be true? Could evolution be at the heart of literally everything? If this is the case, "becoming fit to live" is the sentiment we have every time we take a step forward. And a step forward is always an option.

In the story of "God's Fruit Stand," the woman's mistake is connecting God with something finished. She wants perfect fruit—a completed process. But God is not about perfection. The divine energy initiates and accompanies the drive for perfection; it is not solely associated with the finished product. The divine plants a seed that grows or, to use another metaphor, is a lure that always invites. Therefore, openness to God means that we become a constant unfolding, a never-ceasing development.

I like to think this way because it is both realistic and hopeful in the same breath. It recognizes limit, incompleteness and failure; but it refuses to absolutize these states. There is always a call forward. (This vision plays into the importance of conversion in gospel spirituality. Someone once said, "Conversion is not only the entry into the Christian life, it is the whole thing.")

And you, gentle reader, may be twenty-three or eighty-two, and yet today you have the possibility of leaving an encumbrance behind and striking out on a new path of love. For you are a seed burgeoning toward a ripeness never achieved but always in the process of achieving, a product of God's fruit stand, becoming—in this moment and in every moment to come—"fit to live."

The Grieving Woman and the Spiritual Master

A woman has lost her husband, and she is terribly bereaved. She has tried many remedies from her grief, and finally someone says that she should go see this spiritual master. He will help her with her grief.

So she goes to see him and she tells him about the loss of her husband and how prolonged and difficult her grieving has been.

The spiritual master tells her that he would love to help her, but he is cold. It is a chilly day and he has no wood for his fire. If she would please go and collect some wood and they could build a fire, they could talk without the chill of the day in them. Certainly her terrible grief could be better addressed if both of them were a little warmer.

He asked her to go out and collect some sticks for the fire. There were plenty of houses around where he lived. She should go to each of them and ask for wood. He told her they were very generous people and would surely give it to her.

"But only take wood, please, from a house that has lost no one," the master said.

And so the woman moved from house to house, asking for wood. As she did, however, she had to ask, "If this house has lost no one, then give me some wood."

She came back many hours later without any wood, but with her grief healed.

The saying "No one gets out of life alive" is a flippant attempt to remind us of the universality of suffering and death. Human destiny, however, is not only to suffer and die but to take up an attitude toward suffering and death. In fact, we do not merely undergo anything. We always have to respond to what we undergo. In our capacity to respond lies the possibility of overcoming.

Our response to suffering and death is predictably dichotomous. It either closes us down or opens us up. Often it closes us down at first, makes us feel increasingly isolated. Our loss is so intense that we feel utterly alone. Then, in ways we seldom see coming, the suffering opens us up and puts us in communion with people we have previously ignored. The spiritual healing of suffering begins when it becomes a path to communion with others.

Stephen Levine tells the story of a woman named Hazel. She was suffering with cancer and came into the hospital in "a very contracted state." She was angry and nasty with everyone. The nurses called her "a real bitch on wheels." Then one night, when she was *in especially fierce pain, she just let it all go. A series of profound realizations followed. She joined with what she later called "the ten thousand in pain." She joined with "a brown-skinned woman, breasts slack from malnutrition, a starving child sucking at her empty breast...an Eskimo woman, lying on her side, dying during childbirth...the body of a woman dying by the side of the road after a car accident." Later she said she saw that her pain "wasn't just my pain. It was the pain."*

It is a terrible truth to tell, but suffering often cracks our hardened heart and releases us into the world of suffering where all people at one time or another live.

In her meditation on illness, Susan Sontag said that everyone carries two passports— one to the Kingdom of the Well and the other to the Kingdom of the Sick. Everyone wants to use only one of those passports, but we will all use both. As unpleasant a fact as this is, it may be the way we connect with the human race.

In the movie Ben-Hur, Judah and his fiancée

find his leprous mother and sister and try to bring them to Jesus. They hope that Jesus will heal the two women of their leprosy. When they arrive in Jerusalem, however, Jesus has already been condemned to death and is carrying his cross to Golgatha. They position themselves along the way. Jesus falls to the ground in front of them. The mother tells the guards, "Go easy on that one." The sister also tries to comfort Jesus in his pain.

Judah's fiancée feels her efforts have been futile. "I had hoped...and I brought you here for this." The mother responds, "You haven't failed."

Even though they themselves were suffering and hoped to be cured, the mother and sister reached out to the suffering of another. In doing this they moved out of their isolated pain into the world of shared suffering. They took up their other "passport" and in this simple act there is healing. Later in the story, at the death of Christ, the two were miraculously cured. But they were healed long before they were cured.

The woman in "The Grieving Woman and the

Spiritual Master" cannot be cured. Her husband is irretrievably dead, and loneliness and pain rack her. But perhaps healing is within her reach. She will not find any wood for the fire, for there is no one who has not lost someone. But she may warm herself in a different way. From each person's tale of pain, she will learn she is not alone.

In Christian language, the woman will enter into the body of Christ, where healing and suffering coexist. And, although how healing and suffering coexist is mysterious, the symbol of its truth might well be the phrase "It's not my pain. It's the pain."

The Helper and the Homeless Woman

You might say I'm the gatekeeper here, the first person people meet when they come in for help. My friends at work, they'll call up and say, "St. Peter?" I say, "He's not here right now, can I take a message?"

Anyhow, Family Services is the name of our department. People come in, I direct them to the appropriate office: food, shelter, child protection, welfare, legal services, your basics. My job is to get a sense of who someone is and then find the right place for them.

Not simple.

For a long time I found this an uncomfortable assignment. I don't like sizing up someone according to their problem. It may help them get to the right office, but it also reduces them somehow. Reduces me too. I'll find myself resisting this way of going about things. But I had an experience which changed my way of thinking about it.

There was this woman who was living on the street, one I used to pass on my way to the bus. She was homeless, alcoholic; later it developed she had had a cancer diagnosis. For some reason I decided to take up with her. I liked her smile. Enough of sending everyone elsewhere. I knew the whole maze of social services; I'd take her around myself—clinics, shelters, Medicare, whatever. I guess I wanted to know you could help one person yourself. She was very uncomplaining. Viola. She was willing, even funny about it. "Well, Marie," she'd say, "what are you going to do for me today?"

Oh, the scenes we went through! They called me once from the Women's Shelter. Somehow she'd brought in three pints of Seagram's Seven that night, and a group had gotten drunk. That was against the rules, and I had to take her out. "You told me you'd be good," I said. "You were warm there." She said, "Well, we got warmer."

Or I set her up once with a counselor. After a while he called. "Look, she shows up irregularly, and she always wants to argue with me when she does. What's she here for?" And I'd tell Viola, and she'd say, "Sure, I love to argue with these people. He wants to talk about my childhood all the time. But he doesn't even remember what childhood was like himself. Trust me, Marie."

And I did. I'd have to laugh. She was so insightful and honest. Oh, I really did love her, that one—I really did. But the problems went on for months. Nothing seemed to work out. She kept going back on the street, drinking, getting sicker, all the rest. The more helpless I felt, the more I just loved her; what else could I do? And I'd try again. "Look, Viola," I'd say. "Look where, Marie?" she'd reply. It became a kind of joke between us: "Look," "Look where?"

She moved to a park near my home, and there she started to really go downhill. One evening I went to see her and she was sitting under a tree. She looked awful. I had this powerful feeling that she was getting very close to death. So I went through everything with her one more time: her drinking, her health, her eating, her shelter. She could come live with me. I'd reached that point of willingness.

She just listened, and finally she said, "You know, dear, there's nothing you can do for me anymore." And I saw she was right, I just saw that. And I heaved this big sigh, just let go.

About then, it started raining lightly. I finally said, "Well, it's getting late and wet. Shall we go get some coffee?"

She said, "You go, Marie. I'll be all right here."

I said, "Yeah...well...I'll see you later then." But somehow it felt to both of us like I wouldn't.

I went to the bus, and I was crying on the bus. I felt just brokenhearted. I felt there was something else. I didn't know what. Then this thought came to me that she was out there alone in the rain. Just that. So I got off and took the other bus back and went into the park with a newspaper on my head. I must have looked pretty funny.

She was under the tree. She looked up at me. I sat down. She said, "What are you doing here?" I said, "Nothing, really, I just felt like being with you a little more." She said, "Okay."

So we sat in the rain. There we were. It was relatively dry, because this was a big sycamore tree. I told her about how my father taught me to identify trees by their bark and how I loved trees and nature and felt happiest there. She told me about the desert. She used to live in Arizona. Her favorite place was the desert; it was so peaceful there.

We watched the rain. We watched how the squirrels ran around and the last few people scurrying out. We watched how the park looked with no one in it: some birds, a stray dog....some mist beginning to appear. And I felt finally at peace, and we were both at peace, and we stayed silent a long time. I felt such love.

She walked me to the bus. She said, "Thanks." I said, "For what?" She said, "For nothing." We laughed. "You've been very good to me," she added. We were teary. We hugged. Then I got on the bus, and we waved good-bye. I never saw her again. I'll always love her.

There is a story about a boy scout who was completely possessed by the spirit of helping. He saw an old woman with groceries waiting at a stoplight. He quickly wrested the bag out of her grip, firmly took her arm, and guided her across the street.

As the boy gave the woman back her groceries, she politely said, "Thank you, young man, but I was waiting for the bus. Could we go back across the street now?"

Helping is not as easy as it seems. A cynic once remarked, "Helping is having an inflexible agenda for someone else's life and relentlessly pursuing it." We all fantasize that the world would be better off if people would just let us do for them what we know they need. "People don't know what's good for them" is the remark of someone who is sure he or she does know what's good for other people!

Of course, when things are put so blatantly no one would admit to such flagrant projection. But almost all helpers, at one time or another, have been overeager, pushing their own agenda without seriously consulting the person or people they are supposedly help-ing. This strategy usually leads to frustration. At which point the helper either quits or breaks through to a new level of understanding.

In "The Helper and the Homeless Woman," Marie breaks through. Viola tells her, "You know, dear, there's nothing you can do for me anymore." Marie reflects, "And I saw she was right, I just saw that. And I heaved this big sigh, just let go." Marie sees through her chronic, unrelieved compulsion to have Viola live the life she has arranged for her. She lets go of her own predetermined plans. This opens her to a new possibility.

After she leaves because she doesn't know what to do, she returns just to "be." "She said, 'What are you doing here?' I said, 'Nothing, really. I just felt like being with you a little more.' She said, 'Okay.' "

What ensues is the first equal-to-equal conversation the two women have ever had. They share the things they like and the sights they see. Finally, Viola thanks her for "nothing"— the perfectly appropriate gift of human presence without any self-righteous agendas. Marie has moved from doing what is right for other people whether they like it or not to just accompanying them on the path of their life no matter where that leads.

Quite frankly, I used to like the arrogant style of helping. It makes your ego feel good all over. However, too many of my friends have died. There was no way I could muscle or massage a different outcome. I could not beg a doctor or bully a nurse or make a call that would make everything better. I was reduced to helpless presence. Only gradually did I realize this was not only the best way but the only way—not a reduction but a deepening, a communion beyond omnipotent fantasies.

The
Irritable
Man

I n the spiritual community that G. I. Gurdjieff led in
France, an old man lived who was the per-
sonification of difficulty—irritable, messy, fighting
with everyone, unwilling to clean up or help at all,
and no one got along with him.

Finally, after many frustrating months of trying to stay
with the group, the old man left for Paris. Gurdjieff
quickly followed him and tried to convince him to return, but it had been too hard, and the old man said
no. At last Gurdjieff offered the man a big monthly
stipend if only he'd return.

How could the man refuse? When he returned, however, everyone was aghast, and on hearing that he was being paid (while they were being charged a lot to be there) the community was up in arms.

Gurdjieff called them together and after hearing their complaints he laughed and explained. "This man is like yeast for bread," he said. "Without him you would never really learn about anger, irritability, patience and compassion. That is why you pay me, and that is why I hire him."

The spiritual path may be about finding God. But if it is, it is about finding God at last.

The first discoveries we must make are about that most elusive of quarries—our own selves. For what we know about ourselves is only a fraction of what we actually are. Under normal circumstances, this "fraction" may parade itself as the whole. However, in stressful situ-

ations different—and sometimes shocking—material emerges.

You are sitting in a comfortable chair, reading an inspiring passage about love or compassion or service. You fantasize about the noble life you could lead. "Witness to God in the world," that is who you really are. Motto it on the top of your stationary. Write it on your tombstone.

But then your teenage daughter enters the room with a gripe about her brother (your son), her mother (your wife), her teachers (whom you hoped would ease her transition into young womanhood), her boyfriend (whom you hate), the society (which you worry about), the planet (which you haven't thought about since your third beer last Friday), the universe (which you thought Captain Kirk was in charge of), and (I quote) "the nerd who started it all" (which you suspect is the One whom your grandmother called "the Almighty").

Suddenly, love, compassion and service take a quick holiday. You treat this girl who happens to be your daughter—pardon me, this young woman who has a verifiable genetic connection to you—to a mighty blast from the furnace of the chronically ticked-off.

And even as you say those words you can feel regret dogging every last syllable. It begins to dawn on you that there may be a spiritual learning in all this—but the price, Pilgrim, the price!

Welcome to the world of spirituality. Spiritual consciousness is triggered by conflict which surfaces the hidden "tapes" we all carry around in our minds that engender our attitudes and encourage our behaviors.

These tapes hide. They pretend they don't exist. And as long as harmony reigns in our lives, the pretense goes unchallenged. But once our "button" is pushed, the tapes run. And they drag us down a rock-strewn path and leave us bloody at the end. Of course, we lie about the whole explosion: "I wasn't myself. It will never happen again."

The whole truth is, however, that we were not the self we know. We were the unknown self we also are. We are as much what we do when we "lose it" as when we don't. Gurdjieff said that if you want to study people, do not study psychology. Study mechanics. We all have tapes that are hidden and suddenly triggered by events we do not see coming.

But once we begin to notice these tapes—irritability, anger, pride—we are (at least a little bit) free of them. We can learn the way of non-reactivity, of detachment, of freedom from compulsivity.

We therefore welcome the man who aggravates us, for he teaches us this path of freedom. Bring the man back into the community. Pay him. He brings out into the open exactly what we need to deal with.

They tell the story of two women who every day walked together to a newsstand to buy a paper. The proprietor was always in a bad mood and was ingenious about finding a word or two that could aggravate. Yet one of the women was unfailingly kind to the newsman. No matter how insulting he was, she responded with a kind word. One day her friend said, "How do you do it? Every day this jerk insults you. And every day you treat him well. How do you do it?"

"Why should I let him determine how I act," said the other woman, "and spoil my day?"

Which is why Gurdjieff went after the irritable man in the story, paid him, and honored him with the dubious title "yeast for bread." For in the spiritual life we rise when we recognize the things that make us mindlessly reactive and find the space—albeit ever so small—that allow us to transcend our tapes.

The Jumping Mouse

Once there was a mouse.

He was a busy mouse, searching everywhere, touching his whiskers to the grass, and looking. He was busy as all mice are, busy with mice things. But once in a while he could hear an odd sound. He would lift his head, squinting hard to see, his whiskers wiggling in the air, and he would wonder. One day he scurried up to a fellow mouse and asked him, "Do you hear a roaring in your ears my brother?"

"No, no," answered the other mouse, not lifting his busy nose from the ground. "I hear nothing. I am busy now. Talk to me later."

He asked another mouse the same question and the mouse looked at him strangely. "Are you foolish in your head? What sound?" he asked and slipped into a hole in a fallen cottonwood tree.

The little mouse shrugged his whiskers and busied himself again, determined to forget the whole matter. But there was that roaring again. It was faint, very faint, but it was there! One day he decided to investigate the sound just a little. Leaving the other busy mice, he scurried a little way away and listened again. There it was! He was listening hard when suddenly someone said hello.

"Hello, little brother," the voice said, and Mouse almost jumped right out of his skin. He arched his back and tail and was about to run.

"Hello," again said the voice. "It is I, Brother Raccoon," And sure enough, it was! "What are you doing here all by yourself, little brother?" asked the raccoon. The mouse blushed, and put his nose almost to the ground. "I hear a roaring in my ears and I am investigating it," he answered timidly.

"A roaring in your ears?" replied the raccoon as he sat down with him. "What you hear, little brother, is the river."

"The river?" Mouse asked curiously. "What is a river?"

"Walk with me and I will show you the river," Raccoon said.

Little Mouse was terribly afraid, but he was determined to find out once and for all about the roaring. "I can return to my work," he thought, "after this thing is settled, and possibly this thing may aid me in all my busy examining and collecting. And my brothers all said it was nothing. I will show them. I will ask Raccoon to return with me and I will have proof."

"All right, Raccoon, my brother," said Mouse. "Lead on to the river. I will walk with you."

Little Mouse walked with Raccoon. His little heart was pounding in his breast. The raccoon was taking him upon strange paths and Little Mouse smelled the scent of many things that had gone by this way. Many times he became so frightened he almost turned back. Finally, they came to the river! It was huge and breathtaking, deep and clear in places, and murky in others. Little Mouse was unable to see across it because it was so great. It roared, sang, cried, and thundered on its course. Little Mouse saw great and little pieces of the world carried along on its surface.

"It is powerful!" Little Mouse said, fumbling for words.

"It is a great thing," answered the raccoon, "but here, let me introduce you to a friend."

In a smoother, shallower place was a lily pad, bright and green. Sitting upon it was a frog, almost as green as the pad it sat on. The frog's white belly stood out clearly.

"Hello, little brother," said the frog. "Welcome to the river."

"I must leave you now," cut in Raccoon, "but do not fear, little brother, for Frog will care for you now." And Raccoon left, looking along the river bank for food that he might wash and eat.

Little Mouse approached the water and looked into it.

He saw a frightened mouse reflected there.

"Who are you?" Little Mouse asked the reflection. "Are you not afraid being that far out into the great river?"

"No," answered the frog, "I am not afraid. I have been given the gift from birth to live both above and within the river. When winter man comes and freezes this medicine, I cannot be seen. But all the while thunderbird lives, I am here. To visit me, one must come when the world is green. I, my brother, am the Keeper of the Water.

"Amazing!" Little Mouse said at last, again fumbling for words.

"Would you like to have some medicine power?" Frog asked.

"Medicine power? Me?" asked Little Mouse. "Yes, yes! If it is possible."

"Then crouch as low as you can, and then jump as high as you are able! You will have your medicine!" Frog said.

Little Mouse did as he was instructed. He crouched as low as he could and jumped. And when he did, his eyes saw the Sacred Mountains.

Little Mouse could hardly believe his eyes. But there they were! But then he fell back to earth, and he landed in the river!

Little Mouse became frightened and scrambled back to the bank. He was wet and frightened nearly to death.

"You have tricked me," Little Mouse screamed at the frog.

"Wait," said the frog. "You are not harmed. Do not let your fear and anger blind you. What did you see?"

"I," Mouse stammered, "I, I saw the Sacred Mountains!"

"And you have a new name!" Frog said. "It is Jumping Mouse."

"Thank you. Thank you," Jumping Mouse said, and thanked him again. "I want to return to my people and tell them of this thing that has happened to me."

"Go. Go then," Frog said. "Return to your people. It is easy to find them. Keep the sound of the Medicine River to the back of your head. Go opposite to the sound and you will find your brother mice."

Jumping Mouse returned to the world of the mice. But he found disappointment. No one would listen to him. And because he was wet, and had no way of explaining it because there had been no rain, many of the other mice were afraid of him. They believed he had been spat from the mouth of another animal that had tried to eat him. And they all knew that if he had not been food for the one who wanted him, then he must also be poison for them.

Jumping Mouse lived again among his people, but he could not forget his vision of the Sacred Mountains.

The memory burned in the mind and heart of Jumping Mouse, and one day he went to the edge of the river place....

Jumping Mouse went to the edge of the place of mice and looked out into the prairie. He looked up for eagles. The sky was full of many spots, each one an eagle. But he was determined to go to the Sacred Mountains. He gathered all of his courage and ran just as fast as he could onto the prairie. His little heart pounded with excitement and fear.

He ran until he came to a stand of sage. He was resting and trying to catch his breath when he saw an old mouse. The patch of sage Old Mouse lived in was a haven for mice. Seeds were plentiful and there was nesting material and many things to be busy with.

"Hello," said Old Mouse. "Welcome."

Jumping Mouse was amazed. Such a place and such a mouse. "You are truly a great mouse," Jumping Mouse said with all the respect he could find. "This is truly a wonderful place. And the eagles cannot see you here, either," Jumping Mouse said.

"Yes," said Old Mouse, "and one can see all the beings of the prairie here: the buffalo, antelope, rabbit, and coyote. One can see them all from here and know their names."

"That is marvelous," Jumping Mouse said. "Can you also see the river and the Great Mountains?"

"Yes and no," Old Mouse said with conviction. "I know there is the Great River, but I am afraid that the Great Mountains are only a myth. Forget your passion to see them and stay here with me. There is everything you want here, and it is a good place to be."

"How can he say such a thing?" thought Jumping Mouse. "The medicine of the Sacred Mountains is nothing one can forget."

"Thank you very much for the meal you have shared with me, Old Mouse, and also for sharing your great home," Jumping Mouse said. "But I must seek the mountains."

"You are a foolish mouse to leave here. There is danger on the prairie! Just look up there!" Old Mouse said, with even more conviction. "See all those spots! They are eagles, and they will catch you!"

It was hard for Jumping Mouse to leave, but he gathered his determination and ran hard again. The ground was rough. But he arched his tail and ran with all his might. He could feel the shadows of the spots upon his back as he ran. All those spots! Finally he ran into a stand of chokeberries. Jumping Mouse could hardly believe his eyes. It was cool there and very spacious. There was water, cherries and seeds to eat, grasses to gather for nests, holes to be explored, and many, many other busy things to do. And there were a great many things to gather.

He was investigating his new domain when he heard very heavy breathing. He quickly investigated the sound and discovered its source. It was a great mound of hair with black horns. It was a great buffalo. Jumping Mouse could hardly believe the greatness of the being he saw lying there before him. He was so large that Jumping Mouse could have crawled onto one of his great horns. "Such a magnificent being," thought Jumping Mouse, and he crept closer.

"Hello, my brother," said the buffalo. "Thank you for visiting me."

"Hello, Great Being," said Jumping Mouse. "Why are you lying here?"

"I am sick and I am dying," the buffalo said, "And my medicine has told me that only the eye of a mouse can heal me. But little brother, there is no such thing as a mouse."

Jumping Mouse was shocked. "One of my eyes!" he thought, "One of my tiny eyes." He scurried back into the stand of chokeberries. But the breathing became harder and slower.

"He will die," thought Jumping Mouse, "if I do not give him my eye. He is too great a being to let die."

He went back to where the buffalo lay and spoke. "I am a mouse," he said with a shaky voice. "And you, my brother, are a great being. I cannot let you die. I have two eyes, so you may have one of them."

The minute he had said it, Jumping Mouse's eye flew out of his head and the buffalo was made whole. The buffalo jumped to his feet, shaking Jumping Mouse's whole world.

"Thank you, my little brother," said the buffalo. "I know of your quest for the Sacred Mountains and of your visit to the river. You have given me life so that I may give-away to the people. I will be your brother forever. Run under my belly and I will take you right to the foot of the Sacred Mountains, and you need not fear the spots. The eagles cannot see you while you run under me. All they will see will be the back of a buffalo. I am of the prairie and I will fall on you if I try to go up the mountains."

Little Mouse ran under the buffalo, secure and hidden from the spots, but with only one eye it was frightening. The buffalo's great hooves shook the whole world each time he took a step. Finally they came to a place and Buffalo stopped.

"This is where I must leave you, little brother," said the buffalo.

"Thank you very much," said Jumping Mouse. "But you know, it was very frightening running under you with only one eye. I was constantly in fear of your great earth-shaking hooves."

"Your fear was for nothing," said Buffalo, "for my way of walking is the Sun Dance Way, and I always know where my hooves will fall. I now must return to the prairie, my brother. You can always find me there."

Jumping Mouse immediately began to investigate his new surroundings. There were even more things here than in the other places. Busier things, and an abundance of seeds and other things mice like. In his investigation of these things, suddenly he ran upon a gray wolf who was sitting there doing absolutely nothing.

"Hello, Brother Wolf," Jumping Mouse said.

The wolf's ears came alert and his eyes shone. "Wolf! Wolf! Yes, that is what I am. I am a Wolf!" But then his mind dimmed again and it was not long before he sat quietly again, completely without memory as to who he was. Each time Jumping Mouse reminded him who he was, he became excited with the news, but soon would forget again.

"Such a great being," thought Jumping Mouse, "but he has no memory."

Jumping Mouse went to the center of this new place and was quiet. He listened for a very long time to the beating of his heart. Then suddenly he made up his mind. He scurried back to where the wolf sat and he spoke.

"Brother Wolf," Jumping Mouse said.

"Wolf! Wolf!" said the wolf.

"Please, Brother Wolf," said Jumping Mouse. "Please listen to me. I know what will heal you. It is one of my eyes. And I want to give it to you. You are a greater being than I. I am only a mouse. Please take it.

When Jumping Mouse stopped speaking his eye flew out of his head and the wolf was made whole.

Tears fell down the cheeks of Wolf, but his little brother could not see them, for now he was blind.

"You are a great brother," said the wolf, "for now I have my memory. But now you are blind. I am the guide into the Sacred Mountains. I will take you there. There is a Great Medicine Lake there. The most beautiful lake in the world. All the world is reflected there. The people, the lodges of the people, and all the beings of the prairies and skies."

"Please take me there," Jumping Mouse said.

The wolf guided him through the pines to the Medicine Lake. Jumping Mouse drank the water from the lake. The wolf described the beauty to him.

"I must leave you here," said Wolf, "for I must return so that I may guide others, but I will remain with you as long as you like."

"Thank you, my brother," said Jumping Mouse. "But although I am frightened to be alone, I know you must go so that you may show others the way to this place."

Jumping Mouse sat there trembling in fear. It was no

use running, for he was blind, but he knew an eagle would find him here. He felt a shadow on his back and heard the sound that eagles make. He braced himself for the shock. And the eagle hit! Jumping Mouse went to sleep.

Then he woke up. The surprise of being alive was great, but now he could see! Everything was blurry, but the colors were beautiful.

"I can see! I can see!" said Jumping Mouse over again and again.

A blurry shape came toward Jumping Mouse. Jumping Mouse squinted hard but the shape remained a blur.

"Hello, brother," a voice said. "Do you want some medicine?"

"Some medicine for me?" asked Jumping Mouse. "Yes! Yes!"

"Then crouch down as low as you can," the voice said, "and jump as high as you can."

Jumping Mouse did as he was instructed. He crouched as low as he could and jumped! The wind caught him and carried him higher.

"Do not be afraid," the voice called to him. "Hang on to the wind and trust!"

Jumping Mouse did. He closed his eyes and hung on to the wind and it carried him higher and higher. Jumping Mouse opened his eyes and they were clear, and the higher he went the clearer they became. Jumping Mouse saw his old friend upon a lily pad on the beautiful Medicine Lake. It was the frog.

"You have a new name," called the frog. "You are Eagle."

"The Jumping Mouse" is a wonderful tale of spiritual seeking and developing. Its lessons are many; its insights universal. An entire book of commentary would be appropriate.

One of the things I find striking about the story is how the mouse is never without fear: He is afraid of the sudden appearance of the raccoon, afraid of following the raccoon to the river, afraid after falling into the river, afraid of running out onto the prairie unprotected, afraid of the eagles, afraid of losing an eye, afraid of the buffalo's hooves, afraid waiting by the Medicine Lake, etc.

Yet his fear never stops him.

Fear has a reputation for leading to paralysis. When we are afraid, we recoil. Of course, fear and recoiling are not all bad—without them we would all probably meet with disaster early on. Our physical lives are exceedingly vulnerable, and fear grounded in this sense of vulnerability is on target and keeps us from harm. Be afraid of the hot stove, the speeding car, the high ledge, the big guy's punch...and live to learn about more subtle forms of fear.

We seldom, however, keep fear in its proper and legitimate place. It usually escalates into a primary and ever-present emotion. We create boundaries, and then we allow the boundaries to become barriers. We do not cross our self-imposed boundaries, and whenever we think of crossing them, we become afraid.

We thus find ourselves in a small world hedged in by our own fears. These fears become vigilant, sleepless guards on the walls of the prisons we have made for ourselves.

On occasion, religious rhetoric rides in like the cavalry to liberate us: "Lose your fears. Christ has saved you from fear. Perfect love casts out fear. Trust in God and do not be afraid." Yet our fears are not so easily banished. Even when we have powerful belief systems in place, when divine mercy and love are authentically believed in, we find our fears are still present. Evicting them is no easy matter, no matter how mightily we try.

The story of the jumping mouse suggests a different strategy: Cease fantasizing about eliminating your fears. Learn to live with them in such a way that they do not prohibit your actions.

The mouse's spiritual path began with hearing and seeing the world of spirit that was just beyond his own world and that of his community. Immediately fear arose and he wondered if he should pursue what he had perceived. (Fear lies between recognizing a *possibility and actually pursuing it.)*

But the mouse noticed his fear and took a step. He did not allow his fear to paralyze him. Instead, he moved along and possibility became actuality. The mouse's fear merely came along for the ride.

For him, fear became a companion on his journey, not the master of his barricaded house.

"Junk!"

God bless my mother, and God bless me. We made it through.

She had a stroke and a long period of rehabilitation, and it was clear she was going to have to stay with us for a while. I had all these things in mind: It was a chance to pay her back for all those years. There were these things I was going to help her clear up, like the way she was thinking. I wanted to do the whole job very well, this big opportunity. We should all feel good about it at the end. Little things like that. Some "little"!

Fights? Classics, like only a mother and daughter can have. And my mother is a great fighter, from the Old School of somehow loving it and being very good at it and getting a kind of ecstatic look in your eye when you're really into it. I guess I'm exaggerating. It drives me a little crazy. I hate to argue. Oh, well....

But it got bad. Over a hard-boiled egg we had a bad fight. We'd both gotten worn out, irritable, and frustrated. Boom! I don't remember what about—just about how it was all going, and why her stay had gotten difficult and all of us had become more and more irritable and short-tempered.

In the middle of it, she stopped short and said, "Why are you doing all this for me anyway?" It sort of hit me, and I started to list all the reasons. They just came out: I was afraid for her; I wanted to get her well; I felt maybe I'd ignored her when I was younger; I needed to show her I was strong; I needed to get her ready for going home alone; old age; and on and on. I was amazed myself. I could have gone on giving reasons all night. Even she was impressed.

"Junk," she said when I was done.

"Junk?" I yelled. Like, boy, she'd made a real mistake with that remark. I could really get her.

"Yes, junk," she said again, but a little more quietly. And that little-more-quietly tone got me. And she went on: "You don't have to have all those reasons. We love each other. That's enough."

I felt like a child again. Having your parents show you something that's true, but you don't feel put down—you feel better, because it is true, and you know it, even though you are a child. I said, "You're right. You're really right. I'm sorry." She said, "Don't be sorry. Junk is fine. It's what you don't need any-more. I love you."

It was a wonderful moment, and the fight stopped, which my mother accepted a little reluctantly. No, I'm joking—she was very pleased. She saw how it all was. Everything after that was just, well, easier—less pressure, less trying, less pushing, happening more by itself. And the visit ended up fine. We just spent time together, and then she went back to her house.

The story is told about a man in a morning rush to get to work. As he is leaving the

house, his three-year-old son is playing blocks in front of the door. He steps over him, opens the door, and is well down the front walk when he stops in his tracks. What is he doing? He never plays with his son. He has become a workaholic. Strains of the song "Cat's in the Cradle" play softly in his head.

He turns around and goes back into the house. He throws down his briefcase, rips off his suit coat, and furiously begins to play blocks with his son. After a few minutes, the boy says to him, "Daddy, why are you mad at me?"

Spiritual teachers are concerned with the inner side of outer actions. They stress that sometimes we do things from an inner space of obligation or promise or pride or guilt. We often think the inner side of what we do does not matter and will not show. What is important is that the action get done.

However, there is more to it than that, as any three-year-old can sense. The inner state affects the outer performance. What is going on inside colors what is going on outside. If you play blocks with your son from a conflicted space of anger at yourself and the multiple demands of your life, that anger will affect the play and be quickly picked up. "Daddy, why are you mad at me?" We do not hide our inner selves as well as we think.

The daughter in "Junk" is certainly not hiding it well. She is doing all sorts of things for her ailing mother and it is all going quite badly. All that those "good" outer actions are fomenting is argument. The mother uncovers the problem with a penetrating question, "Why are you doing all this for me anyway?" From what space in you is all this action coming from? There is no shortage of reasons from the daughter and, at first glance, they seem to represent the opening of a floodgate of concern. But a closer look reveals they are coming from ego, anxiety, apprehension and guilt.

The mother's response is that her daughter's motivations are all "junk." There is another level where action can flow from—love. There will always be junk, but when love becomes the source of action, junk is "what you don't need anymore." The actions that flow from love are "well, easier—less pressure, less try-

ing, less pushing, happening more by itself." In Christian language, when we do things out of love, grace is present and the human will is riding it out into the world. While we are doing it, it is getting done.

To act out of love is to incarnate spirit. Whatever you are doing—diapering a baby, making linguine a la vongole, cutting the grass, doing homework—becomes spirit-suffused activity. To incarnate spirit is what we are all meant to do. What is often not said is that spirit wants to be incarnate; its nature is to unfold itself in action. So if we but touch spirit, we are on the way to enfleshing it.

There is no mistaking when spirit is guiding us. Things are happening "well, easier—less pressure, less trying, less pushing, happening more by itself." This is the "easy yoke" that Jesus urged people to put on.

The Legend
of the Bells

The temple had stood on an island two miles out
to sea. And it held a thousand bells. Big bells,
small bells, bells fashioned by the best crafts-
men in the world. When a wind blew or a storm raged,
all the temple bells would peal out in unison, produc-
ing a symphony that sent the heart of the hearer into
raptures.

But over the centuries the island sank into the sea
and, with it, the temple and the bells. An ancient
tradition said that the bells continued to peal out,
ceaselessly, and could be heard by anyone who listened attentively. Inspired by this tradition, a young
man travelled thousands of miles, determined to hear
those bells. He sat for days on the shore, opposite

the place where the temple had once stood, and listened—listened with all his heart. But all he could hear was the sound of the waves breaking on the shore. He made every effort to push away the sound of the waves so that he could hear the bells. But all to no avail; the sound of the sea seemed to flood the universe.

He kept at his task for many weeks. When he got disheartened he would listen to the words of the village pundits who spoke with unction of the legend of the temple bells and of those who had heard them and proved the legend to be true. And his heart would be aflame as he heard their words...only to become discouraged again when weeks of further effort yielded no results.

Finally he decided to give up the attempt. Perhaps he was not destined to be one of those fortunate ones who heard the bells. Perhaps the legend was not true. He would return home and admit failure. It was his final day, and he went to his favorite spot on the shore to say goodbye to the sea and the sky and the wind and the coconut trees. He lay on the sands, gazing up at the sky, listening to the sound of the sea. He did not resist that sound that day. Instead, he gave himself over to it and found it was a pleasant, soothing sound, this roar of the waves. Soon he became so lost in the sound that he was barely conscious of himself, so deep was the silence that the sound produced in his heart.

In the depth of that silence, he heard it! The tinkle of a tiny bell followed by another, and another and another...and soon every one of the thousand temple bells was pealing out in glorious unison, and his heart was transported with wonder and joy.

Young men believe the legends of tradition. They follow them to the edge of islands and listen out into the restless sea. Traditions can seduce us into adventure. They can break into our gray worlds with technicolor news.

This is not the usual "take" on tradition. It is commonly thought that traditions are either blessings or burdens. If they are blessings, it is because they provide touchstones for identity. They stabilize us in turbulent times. Without traditions, "We would be as shaky as a fiddler on a roof." If traditions are burdens, it is because they are inheritances from a past that no longer is. They refuse newness, resist change, stifle initiative.

In this story, however, tradition flies much higher. The tradition carries inside it the very possibility of experience. It states the conditions under which certain wonderful things may happen. "An ancient tradition said that the bells continued to peal out, ceaselessly, and could be heard by anyone who listened attentively." The tradition is a map—cryptic, to be sure—but still a map to spiritual discoveries. And when the young man becomes disheartened, it is the legend itself—enshrined in tradition—that keeps him going. Thus traditions provide both the direction and heart for spiritual seekers.

But young men who believe in traditions and heed their call often do not know how to follow their instructions. They think "listening attentively" means screening out distractions. The initial mistake the young man makes is to think the sound of the sea is competing with the sound of the bells and that what he must do is eliminate the sound of the sea so the sound of the bells will emerge.

He is not alone in this mistake. We often pursue God by not pursing the world. But if we know how to listen, the world mediates the divine voice; it does not obscure it. When the young man finally gives himself to the sound of the sea, he paradoxically enters a silence where the thousand temple bells peal.

We do not step over creation to get to God. We enter into creation and find the divine as its inner radiance. To listen attentively means to hear the temple bells through *the roaring of the sea, not despite it.*

Nikos Kazantzakis, the Greek poet and novelist, was fond of this quick spiritual exchange: "The monk said, 'Sister almond tree, speak to me of God.' And the almond tree blossomed."

The young man on the beach, being rung by the ringing of the temple bells, knows the truth of the almond tree.

Lord Krishna and the Two Kings

Lord Krishna wanted to test the wisdom of his kings. One day he summoned a king named Duryodana. Duryodana was well known throughout his kingdom for his cruelty and miserliness, and his subjects lived in terror. Lord Krishna said to King Duryodana, "I want you to go and travel the world over and find for me one truly good man." Duryodana replied, "Yes, Lord," and obediently began his search. He met and spoke with many people, and after much time had passed he returned to Lord Krishna saying, "Lord, I have done as you have asked and searched the world over for one truly good man. He is not to be found. All of them are selfish and wicked. Nowhere is there to be found this good man you seek!"

Lord Krishna sent him away and called another king named Dhammaraja. He was a king well known for his generosity and benevolence and well loved by all his people. Krishna said to him, "King Dhammaraja, I wish for you to travel the world over and bring to me one truly wicked man." Dhammaraja also obeyed, and on his travels met and spoke with many people. After much time had passed he returned to Krishna saying, "Lord, I have failed you. There are people who are misguided, people who are misled, people who act in blindness, but nowhere could I find one truly evil man. They are all good at heart despite their failings!"

" 'Breakfast for the mind' is what I call it," the woman smiled.

In my lecture I had mentioned that many spiritual teachers stress putting something beautiful in your mind at the start of each day by meditating on an inspiring spiritual passage.

In this way you install a "beauty detector," and throughout the day you notice all the beautiful things you come across.

Our awareness is very selective. In general, we notice what we set our receptors for and we miss in the outer world what is first missing in the inner world. In the Sermon on the Mount, the Matthean Jesus says, "Blessed are the single-hearted, they shall see God." The single-hearted are those who have quieted their minds and deeply focused themselves. Their awareness rests in the soul space, where our deepest selves open into the world of spirit. In this space we become what we call the image of God or the child of God. When we are in this space—connected to the divine life—we look out and see all other things connected to God. As the Talmud says, "You do not see things as they are. You see things as you are."

This is the controlling secret of both Duryodana and Dhammaraja. Duryodana is known for his cruelty and miserliness. Therefore, when he is sent in search of a good man, he can find none. The features of evil are so powerfully established in his mind that they prohibit him from seeing goodness. Dhammaraja is a man of generosity and benevolence. Therefore, when he looks for an evil man, he can find none. The features of goodness are so powerfully established in his mind that they prohibit him from seeing evil.

Where does "Lord Krishna and the Two Kings" leave us? Are we mere victims of our conditioning? Do we see only what we have been programmed to see? Is there no truth, only relative filters?

Answers to these questions could take us into philosophy and psychology, but Christianity has a more practical approach: Put on the mind of Christ. With his mind we will see the intimate struggle between good and evil and the Beauty that underlies it, a Beauty even the gates of hell cannot prevail against.

That is more than breakfast for the mind. That is a feast for the human spirit.

The Man on the Ox

A monk rode an ox into town and came to a group of people.

The people asked him, "What are you looking for, monk?"

He said, "I am looking for an ox."

They all laughed.

He rode his ox to the next group of people. They asked him, "What are you looking for, monk?"

He said, "I am looking for an ox."

They all laughed.

He rode his ox to a third group of people. They asked him, "What are you looking for, monk?"

He said, "I am looking for an ox."

They said, "This is ridiculous. You are a man riding an ox looking for an ox!"

The monk said, "So it is with you looking for God."

My doctoral dissertation was entitled Religious Language in a Secular Culture in the Thought of Langdon Gilkey. *While I was writing it, I was having trouble with some sections of Gilkey's writing. I called him up to talk about it. I can't remember exactly what I said to him, but I clearly remember what he said to me: "God isn't a great green bird, you know."*

Somehow in the way I was talking I was giving Gilkey the impression that I believed God was an object in the world—a rare object, an exotic object, but nevertheless an object. But God is not an object in the world, and any search for God that puts him/her/it in the same general category as lost car keys is fundamentally mistaken.

It is, however, an easy mistake to make. The very way we talk practically forces it. We make "God" a noun and then use it as the subject and object of sentences. "God" does this or that; we pray to "God" or seek after "God." Now, nouns name discrete entities in the world—persons, places, things. So when we make "God" a noun, we can easily get the idea that "God" is a discrete entity to be found somewhere in the world. So, as Sherlock Holmes might say, "The game's afoot!" Let the search for God begin.

Spiritual teachers like to discourage this search. Many of their teachings hope to redirect us and open us to the real presence of God.

"When will the Kingdom of God come?" asked

the Pharisees. "You cannot see the Kingdom of God by observation," replied Jesus. "If they say, 'Lo, there it is!' or 'Lo, here it is!' do not believe them. The Kingdom of God is within you."

Other spiritual teachers say the same thing in different ways:

> "You would not be searching for God if God had not already found you."

> "There is no such thing as a search for God, for there is nothing in which God cannot be found."

> "Dear God, it is not you who is missing, it is I."

God is not one more thing but that which sustains all things. The divine is the spiritual dimension that suffuses all reality. It is always present, but we are not always attuned to that presence. We do not know how to attend to it. This is one of the reasons the Buddha said, "Don't just do something, stand there." Doing things within our normal framework is not helpful in finding God. We must reconceive the whole enterprise.

But, of course, changing consciousness is no easy task. We are addicted to the usual structures of awareness and the types of searches they initiate.

Once a man lost his car keys and was looking for them under a streetlight. Another man came and asked what he was doing.

"Looking for my keys."

"I'll help."

The two men searched for the keys but had no luck. After a while the helper asked, "Where did you lose the keys?"

"Inside the house," the seeker said.

"Then why are we looking out here?"

"The light's better," the seeker explained.

We tend to do what we are comfortable with, even when something totally different is called for. We look in the light because we can see better there, even when what we have lost is in darkness.

But never mind all this theological stuff.

Ride that ox, Monk.

God is right around the next corner.

Nasrudin and the Hot Peppers

Nasrudin loved to point out to people the endless way of human foibles.

Once, he sat in the marketplace on a busy marketday. Next to him was a basket of hot peppers.

Nasrudin popped one into his mouth, and then popped a second and then a third. By the time he had popped a fourth, a sweat had broken out on his forehead. He began to perspire slightly and his face began to turn red. His mouth was open and his tongue was hanging out.

Then he began to cry out, "Oh, God, these peppers

are killing me!"

Then he took another pepper and popped it into his mouth. "Oh, God," he screamed, "I can't handle it. These peppers are killing me!"

The sweat began to pour down Nasrudin's face. His clothes were soaked with perspiration. But another pepper went in his mouth.

"Oh, God, Oh, God," he yelled. "I can't take it, I can't take it!"

Another hot pepper went in and he kept pouring the hot peppers into his mouth one after another, all the while screaming out in pain, "Oh, my God, these peppers are killing me!"

A crowd of people had gather around him and they finally asked him, "Nasrudin, Nasrudin, why do you not stop eating the peppers?"

He said, "I'm hoping to find a sweet one."

A friend of mine is fond of saying, "We avoid with a passion the things that will save us."

This story suggests a flip side to that strange human penchant: "We embrace with a passion the things that are killing us."

One more hot pepper, please!

One of the tastier hot peppers we "enjoy" is the belief that possessions will satisfy us and bring us the inner peace that we seek. So we accumulate—cars, watches, televisions, homes, etc. Now, most of us are not new to this accumulation game. We know from past experience that most of the things we lust after and pursue will eventually become part of a garage sale. They will not permanently quench our thirst or satisfy our appetite. However, this does not stop us. We keep on popping down the peppers—hoping, like Nasrudin, to find a sweet one.

Another appetizing pepper is the habit of judging people by appearance. We look at a beautiful body and assume a scintillating personality and high moral character. Then we see a squat body and assume it encases a boring couch potato. We observe an old person or a young one or a city denizen or a suburbanite and we begin to salivate with a whole series of judgments. We know from experience that these judgments are usually incorrect. We say with amazement, "He's not as dumb as he looks!" It seldom dawns on us that this is more a comment on our prejudgment than the person's intelligence. Yet on and on we go, judging by appearances, gulping down one hot pepper after another with nary a sweet one to justify the exercise.

Spiritual teachers constantly point out these and many other "peppers" that are patently bad for us. We say, "You are right. That's very insightful. I'll eat two."

There is such a thing as persistent human folly, and every person's diet includes at least one dish of hot peppers.

Nasrudin and the Perfect Woman

A disciple asked Nasrudin, "Why did you never marry?"

Nasrudin said, "When I was younger I was in search of the perfect woman, and in Cairo I met a woman. She was beautiful and intelligent, but unkind.

"And in Baghdad I met a woman. She was generous and gracious, but we had nothing in common.

"This happened again and again and again, until finally I met a woman who was perfect. We had everything in common. She was generous, gracious, beautiful, intelligent...."

The disciple asked, "Then why did you not marry her?"

"Well," said Nasrudin, "it was sad. You see, she was looking for the perfect man."

A hundred years ago when I was a seminarian, I was working in a parish during the summer and was invited to have dinner with the priests. During dinner one of the priests said that he had lunch with a Bill somebody. The other priests asked how Bill was doing.

"Fine. He got a B and we were celebrating it."

"How's he handling it?" one of the priests asked.

"Pretty good. Life goes on even after a B."

"But B is a good grade," I volunteered.

"Not for Bill," the priests said and laughed.

It turned out that Bill was in fourth year of high school and had never gotten anything but an A. He was bright, but his high grades were the hard work of a "grade-grubber." Bill was going through life tortured by his own perfectionism. Getting a few low grades and learning how to live with them were the path of his salvation.

Perfectionism is a true torturer. It makes us overlook the beauty of things and concentrate on their flaws. Nothing is ever good enough and we feel obliged to comment on every failure. When we are gripped by perfectionism, anything that goes wrong completely spoils the whole enterprise. We are hard on ourselves and on others.

I remember a story that was told to me about a man who got sick while traveling in Italy and had to be hospitalized. When the nurse helped him slip the hospital gown over his head, it proved too small and split over and under both shoulders. The nurse stepped back, took a long look, and said, "Che elegante!" ("How elegant!") This nurse's vocation in life was to erase any trace of perfectionism in her patients.

Perfectionism is obviously a psychological problem. But it can also be interpreted from a spiritual perspective. The human person is a boundary creature, living along the border of spirit and matter. This hybrid reality of transcendence and finitude, of being in the world but not of the world, causes tension. We often collapse the tension on the side of matter and insist that is what we are and no more. This is the error of materialism. Or we can collapse the tension on the side of spirit. This is the error of "angelism," and angelism is the spiritual perspective that breeds perfectionism.

Angelism refuses to acknowledge that we are finite, particular, limited beings. These limits are not an accident or temporary restraints that will be removed by death. The particularity of our being is essential to who we are. We are incarnate spirits or, to flip it, enspirited matter. The spirit side of us is continually seeking expression in matter and the matter side of us is continually opening itself to spirit. Angelism does not like pure spirit immersed and expressed in messy matter. It wants perfection, and things like minds and bodies are too concrete to provide it.

If perfection is tied to angelism, both should be rejected. For incarnate spirits, the search for perfection is replaced by the process of conversion. We are constantly "reaching within" to touch a love that is resourced by the divine spirit and then "going out" into the world with that love, using the limitations of our mind and the clumsiness of our bodies. Of course, we never fully incarnate that love, and so we are always caught in the flow between spirit and matter. But when we understand this truth about our non-perfect natures, we paradoxically enter the only perfection we are capable of—to humbly accept and live within the human process of spirit enlivening matter.

Nasrudin wants the perfect wife. He is looking for an angel. When he finds her, no marriage is possible, for she too is looking for an angel. As Jesus said in another context, angels neither marry nor are given in marriage. However, on earth imperfect men and women are constantly looking for flesh-and-

blood companions who are comfortable with the process of incarnating love.

The Obedient and the Disobedient Servants

A king had two servants. He told the first servant to do something. The servant did it and was promoted. He told the second servant to do something. The servant did not do it and was fired.

The servant who was promoted lived very, very well in the king's service and continued to obey the king and be promoted. One day, however, his thoughts turned to the servant who had disobeyed the king and been fired. So he went to visit him.

He arrived at the house where the man used to live, but he was no longer there. A neighbor said he had sold the house and moved to a much smaller one.

When the first servant arrived at the place where the second servant now lived, he realized that "house" was too kind a word. It was a hovel. The first servant knocked on the door, and a voice said, "Come in."

The second servant was sitting on the dirt floor eating a very, very thin soup.

The servant who had been promoted smiled. "If you had learned to obey the king, you would not have to eat that thin soup," he said.

The servant who had been fired said, "If you had learned how to eat thin soup, you would not have to obey the king!"

The structure of this story is very similar to the structure of many of Jesus' parables. The

*story gets us going one way, reinforcing con-
ventional wisdom, and then at the end there
is a sudden reversal that invites us to consider everything from a different point of
view. We are sucked in and surprised. We
might just feel bamboozled by the whole tale
and walk away from it. Or we may become
intrigued by the switch and begin to puzzle
out the new way of seeing that is being pro-
posed to us.*

*Obedience to the king is rewarded; disobe-
dience is punished. What else is new? The
obedient servant is obviously in a good position and, as the story unfolds, the disobedient servant has fallen on hard times—loss
of employment and housing, forced to eat
meager meals. The obedient servant wants
to lay the blame for all this on the disobedient servant's behavior. And, if we are honest, so do we. This guy brought it on himself.*

*The last line is a shocker, however. It is not
the disobedient servant who is in spiritual
trouble. He has stayed faithful to himself,
even at the cost of losing food, shelter and
work. He will tolerate lesser physical conditions as long as he remains free to disobey*

the king. The burden of investigation shifts to the obedient servant. Has he compromised his integrity for material things? Which servant is in good spiritual shape and which is in bad? In gospel language, which one goes home justified?

"The Obedient and the Disobedient Servants" reminds me of a startling scene in the Gospel of Luke. Jesus, having been severely beaten, is carrying his cross to Golgatha to be crucified. The women of Jerusalem, seeing this horrible sight, weep for him. He quickly corrects their crying: They should weep for themselves and for their children. There is nothing wrong with him. He is only dying. But he has not lost touch with his "Abba." He is in life-giving contact with God, and that is what is most important. Everything else to Jesus is secondary to the protection and nurture of this relationship. The women, symbolizing the people of Jerusalem, are out of touch with the reality of God. Their tears should be for themselves and their alienated condition. The people who appear in good shape are really in bad shape, and the one who looks in terrible shape is really in perfect shape.

We, of course, want it both ways. We want to obey the king and enhance our work, shelter and food, yet we do not wish to compromise ourselves in any way whatsoever. May that always be the case!

Spiritual teachers, however, like to draw sharp contrasts. They want to force the questions of priorities and what will be sacrificed for what. To them, in a world where the path of success often entails the loss of inner integrity, a simple "I won't do it" may be the sign of someone really at peace.

And when that person suffers the consequences of his or her refusal, many of us will look and say, "Poor man" or "Poor woman" and "What can you expect when you won't go along?" Of course, we will fail to perceive our own real poverty or the disobedient one's true wealth.

Paint the
Other Side

Claire and Tom were going to be married twenty-five years on Friday. They decided against a party. They had a slew of good reasons. Whom to invite, where to have it, how to be serious about not wanting gifts. Besides, it would cost a fortune.

A week earlier Claire, suspicious that her sister Ann might be cooking up something, had phoned her with their decision. "Tom and I will probably just go out to dinner." Then she added the obligatory, "A candle-light dinner." There was silence on the other end. "So no surprises. O.K., Ann?"

More silence. Then, "Caught my thought, did you? Well, O.K. If that's the way you two want it."

From the tone of her sister's voice Claire knew she had surprised her. Ann had not given the anniversary a thought until Claire mentioned it. She had been the maid of honor, too.

The lone voice for a party was Joyce, their eighteen-year-old daughter. The single reason which she put forward—as if it would change everything—was, "It only happens once." This observation left Tom and Claire speechless. "Well," Claire finally said, reaching into the storehouse of stock parental responses, "your father and I have already decided."

"Jeez," said Joyce. "You'd think it was a burden."

Claire got sick Thursday night and spent Friday on the sofa in a housecoat with a box of Kleenex. She blew her nose, watched soaps, and pondered.

When Tom got home from work, he took one look at her curled up on the sofa, her nose red, her face without expression. "Psychosomatic?" he ventured.

"Why can't we get worked up for this, Tom? It only happens once."

"Is there something wrong with us?" Tom said to the air between them.

"Not that I know of." Claire pushed her hair back.

"Me neither." Tom plopped into the chair he had plopped into every evening for twenty-five years. "Well, maybe this is just how it is after twenty-five years."

"Oh God," sighed Claire at the prospect of this blah extending indefinitely into the future. It was the first real prayer she had uttered in years.

"Surprise!" Joyce jumped from the hallway. In her hands was a rectangular box wrapped with anniversary paper.

"It looks like a half-gallon of booze to me," Tom said. "Maybe we should stay home and get drunk."

"Wrong!" said Joyce.

Next came an operatic "Happy Anniversary" accompanied by a dance that combined ballet and bugaloo. On the final chord Joyce deposited the box in Claire's lap. The Kleenex was snatched away.

Claire opened the card. On the cover was an unshaven man in T-shirt, baggy pants, and slippers, plopped down in front of the T.V. His right hand held a can of beer which rested on his potbelly. At the other end of the sofa was a woman in curlers, face cream, and housecoat, darning a sock. Her finger stuck through a hole in the sock and she was staring stupidly at it. The inscription read: "To a still handsome man and a still beautiful woman on their silver anniversary."

Claire glared at Joyce.

"Look inside, Mom."

Inside was a picture of a teenage girl, ratty hair, braces, freckles, pimples, jeans with a hole in the knee, and a T-shirt which read, "Puke!" The inscription read: "From your still beautiful daughter."

Claire let out a "short snort," which is what Tom calls "her laugh when she is trying not to." She passed the card to Tom.

"I don't remember posing for this," he said, staring at the potbellied man on the front.

"Wrong!" said Joyce. "Open it, Mom."

Claire carefully unwrapped the box and unlatched its notched cardboard top.

"What is this?" she exclaimed as she pulled out the tissue-wrapped object.

"Careful, Mom."

In Claire's hands was a large, Waterford crystal vase.

The last light of the day was streaming through the west window. It caught the vase and reflected along each cut of the glass. The sun danced on the crystal.

"Oh God, it's beautiful," said Claire softly.

Tom was stunned. He could think of nothing to say, so he said, "Where did you get the money?"

"I robbed a bank."

"What? No flowers?" was his comeback.

Joyce disappeared. Tom reached for the Kleenex.

Joyce was back as quickly as she left. In her hands were yellow mums. She put them on the table, ran into the kitchen, filled the gravy pitcher with water, and poured the water in the vase. She arranged the flowers one by one and fluffed them carefully.

"Renoir or Matisse or somebody says you must carefully arrange flowers," Joyce instructed. She put the vase on the table between the sofa where her mother was and the chair her father sat in.

"Then when you are done," she continued, "you turn the flowers around and paint the other side." She turned the vase around so that Tom and Claire both saw the side that was hidden from them. "There,"

Joyce said.

"Who told you that?" Tom asked.

"My art teacher."

"Smart man that Renoir or Matisse or somebody."

"Come here," said her mother. Claire kissed her.

"Thanks, darling. It means more than you know."

"My turn," said Tom. Joyce came over and sat in her father's lap. He kissed her nose like he used to when she was a little girl. "That last eighteen were the best of the twenty-five," he said.

"I agree," said Claire.

For a long time they all looked at the vase. There did not seem to be a need to say anything.

Finally, Claire bounced up from the sofa. "Make reservations for three at someplace expensive. I'm going to get dressed."

She walked down the hall to her bedroom; and from the view her husband and daughter had, it looked like her housecoat lifted off the floor with each step.

"Is Mom skipping?" asked Joyce incredulously.

"Your mother always skips," said the man who had been married twenty-five years.

Our inner lives do not always follow the outer calendar. We can feel joyless at Christmas, hopeless at Easter, suicidal on our birthday, and even question whether we took the right path on our twenty-fifth anniversary. But if we insist on having the appropriate emotions and perspectives first, we might never celebrate.

The story is told of a monastery that was severely divided. In this state of division the monks decided that they should not celebrate the Eucharist. They argued that the Eucharist was a sign of unity and since there was no unity among them, they could not and would not celebrate. Finally, it was pointed out to the monks that the Eucharist was an eschatological *sign of unity, that is, it cel-ebrated a unity that would come about com-pletely only in the future. By celebrating this future unity we give notice to the divisive present that it will not last. So with their con-sciousness raised the monks were able to enter into the liturgy, and—lo and behold— their divisions were gradually bridged and their wounds healed.*

The normal way is to achieve an inner state of peace and then do the peaceful thing, or to feel joy and gratitude and then do the joy-ous and grateful thing. But often we have to do it the other way around. We perform a peaceful act and an inner peace comes about. Or we act happy or thankful and discover in-ner joy and gratitude have become a reality.

Tom and Claire in "Paint the Other Side" can-not get worked up for their twenty-fifth wed-ding anniversary. Their eighteen-year-old daughter, Joyce, cannot get worked down. She knows the value of the moment. "It only happens once," she reminds them. Although she was not there for the entire twenty-five years, she is going to celebrate it with mu-sic, dance and gifts—even if the celebration has to be held in the midst of her parents' glumness.

But Joyce's joy, humor and sensitivity are seductive. New feelings begin to emerge in Tom and Claire as they see their married life through the eyes of their daughter. At first they are dragged into celebrating their anniversary by their bouncy daughter. But by the end Claire is also bouncing and Tom thinks that is the way she always is. The inner world and the outer calendar have come together. Tom and Claire have learned to paint the other side. And it is not "Renoir or Matisse or somebody" who has taught them.

> We all need a Joyce in our lives,
> someone dedicated to celebrating,
> who is not put off by contrary moods,
> who declares every resistant impulse
>   "Wrong!"
> who continues in her joyous acts
> until even the most reluctant heart skips.

The Prince and the Monkey

A prince and many of his archers went out to hunt monkeys. They became separated in the woods and the prince was by himself when he saw a monkey high in a tree.

The prince took an arrow from his quiver, put it in his bow, aimed it carefully at the monkey, and let it fly.

The monkey's ears perked up when he heard the twang of the bow. He turned around and as the arrow sped toward him the monkey calmly stepped to one side and grabbed it in midair.

The prince was astounded. He applauded the monkey.

Then the prince took another arrow from his quiver, put it in his bow, aimed it carefully at the monkey, and let it fly.

The monkey stepped to the other side and caught the arrow in his other hand.

The prince was astounded. He applauded the monkey again.

Then the monkey put both arrows in one of his hands, turned around, wriggled his rear end, and laughed mockingly, "Na-Na-Na-Na-Na-Na!"

The prince then called up all his archers, and they riddled the monkey with arrows.

"I don't get it," she said.

"Stay with it," I said.

It was the first day of a two-day workshop on

storytelling and spiritual development. I had just told "The Prince and the Monkey," and not a lot of lightbulbs had gone on, including this woman's

The next day she returned and immediately cornered me. "I told that story to my twelve-year-old son last night and he laughed out loud. I asked him why he laughed and he said, 'That's what you get for showing off.' "

The boy's response seems more appreciative of the story than the man in the class who suggested this moral: "Two arrows in the hand is better than forty in the butt."

I had not heard the phrase "showing off" in a long time. But it had been commonplace in my growing up. To be called a "show-off" was a serious charge. It was a moral disorder of major magnitude.

But it is difficult to spell out what exactly is wrong with the show the monkey puts on.

Upon first analysis, showing off is doing things to be seen, noticed, known rather than do-ing them for the pleasure of doing them.

This may be at least part of the inner life of the monkey. However, it is not revealed until the end of the story. Things seem to be going splendidly until the monkey decides to flaunt his skills. When he is exercising his abilities without any self-consciousness, the prince is appreciative. When the monkey suddenly starts taunting the prince, the prince responds in kind. Only the prince has arrows at his command.

The monkey's final "Na-Na-Na-Na-Na-Na!" shows not only that he was exercising his skills to be seen but that he was exercising his skills to "put down" the prince. The monkey thinks highly of himself and very little of the prince. His skills are brought forward not in the pursuit of excellence but in the pursuit of domination. Showing up the prince is the flip side of showing off himself. It is the sudden revelation of this attitude that changes the course of the story and brings about the monkey's downfall.

Could it be that these twin sides of showing off—wanting to be seen and wanting to dominate—undercut the natural flow of our excellence?

Everyone has skills and abilities, and everyone has to compete. The question raised by this story is: How do we relate to our own skills and with what attitude do we enter into the world of competition?

The next time you watch a football game and they are "strutting their stuff" in the end zone after a touchdown with an "in-your-face" attitude toward the defenders they have just beaten, think of the monkey.

Na-Na-Na-Na-Na-Na!

The Rock

The teacher decided that during the first three days of Holy Week the eighth grade class would put on a passion play. There would be six performances with different grades attending each performance. In this way the eighth graders would learn the passion according to St. Matthew and so would the entire school.

It seemed like a good idea.

As often happens with good ideas, there were a few snags. There were more eighth graders than there were parts in the passion play or the need for stage hands, set designers, etc. So the teacher succumbed to another good idea—to move in the direction of imaginative, *avant-garde* theater. She cast every animate and inanimate reference in Matthew. She cast:

- the tree from which Judas hanged himself,
- the broken vase of perfume,
- five people simulating an earthquake,
- three people doing a credible job of imitating thirty clattering pieces of silver on the temple floor,
- bystanders,
- more bystanders,
- still more bystanders.

She also cast the rock that blocked the entrance to the tomb of Jesus. This was not a difficult task; it was a matter of typecasting. There was a boy who had, as his mother put it, "sprouted early." He was definitely bigger than a bread box. He was also, bent over with his hands clasping his ankles, a perfect boulder.

"John," the teacher said, "you will be the rock—the one blocking the tomb, not the Apostle Peter. (Teachers cannot avoid puns, especially when they are teaching religion.)

For the Angel of the Lord, who pushes the rock aside, she chose the most petite girl in the class—Tinkerbell one size up. The contrast, the teacher felt, was positively biblical.

The first performance was for the third grade. The play was predictably moving along with the usual sniggers and laughs until the Angel of the Lord appeared. With her little finger outstretched, she nudged the rolled up rock. He somersaulted away from the entrance of the tomb, staying perfectly rolled up. Then the angel sat on him, making the stone of death the throne of the Lord—just as it says in the Gospel of Matthew.

The audience went wild. They cheered and chanted, "Rock! Rock! Rock!" Afterwards they swarmed him for autographs. He modestly signed, "Rock." This happened at performance after performance.

Thus a star was born.

Also a critic. The teacher was not sure all this attention was good for the Rock. Perhaps the glory should be shared. She took the Rock aside and suggested that he play the tree from which Judas hangs himself. Someone else should have a chance at being the rock. The Rock said he did not think this was a good idea. "I like being the rock," he said.

The teacher responded (with what she later thought was the best question of her career), "Why?"

"I like letting Christ out of the tomb," the Rock said.

"But, John, the rock isn't rolled back so Christ can get out. He is already gone." (Teachers are always quick to correct.) "The rock," she pointed out, "is rolled back so that the women can see in."

The Rock's face twisted as he floundered for the first time in the deep waters of the spirit. "Well," he said, "how did he get out if the rock was still stuck in the hole?"

This is the type of question all teachers fear. There is an answer, but it is light years beyond what the questioner is able to handle. The teacher remained silent, searching for words. But the Rock found the words before the teacher did.

"Well," he said, "I guess huge rocks are no big thing for God."

Thus did the Rock roll back the boulder from his own mind and see into the empty darkness of the Easter revelation.

The teacher said in a quiet, choking voice that he should continue in the role of the rock, since he knew the part so well.

Almost everyone who becomes interested in the spiritual life and tries to pursue it falls by the wayside. Jesus' parable of the sower and the seed suggests that most of the seed meets with hard times—carried off by alien forces, withering from lack of roots, choked by anxiety, etc. This does not have to be a permanent fate, however. We can return to the path of spiritual development or, as in the gospel image, find better soil for the wild seed-scattering of God.

But how do we do that?

"The Rock" suggests that we meditate on the fact that "Huge rocks are no big thing for God." The truth hidden in this symbolic sentencing can entice us back into considering the world of spirit. It is meant to blow our minds, to undermine the certainty of our ordinary level of consciousness.

What we think is the case and has to be the

case may not be the case at all. Things are not what they seem. They are more than they seem. Huge rocks may not be the obstacles they appear. The common sense approach to life ("How did he get out if the rock was still stuck in the hole?") does not define reality. The Scriptures capture this perspective in the phrase, "With humans it is impossible, but with God all things are possible."

The universe is an open-ended reality. However, our minds close it off with remarkable regularity. When we begin to see this and take seriously the fact that what we are aware of is only a fraction of what is, we are back on the spiritual path—back to the good soil. We begin to relativize our cherished ideas and make room for the larger mystery within which we live and move and have our being. Things are not so tight anymore, and we move away from the routine and the predictable toward the realm of adventure.

The teacher and the boy both appreciate the transcendent truth of resurrection. But they approach it from different perspectives. The teacher focuses on what people will see when they look into the tomb. They will see noth-

ing. Death is empty. It cannot hold Christ. There is nothing in tombs. Visit them if you will, but be prepared for the question, "Why do you seek the living among the dead?"

The boy, on the other hand, focuses on what must happen in order for people to see in. A huge rock must be rolled away. The rock is our attachment to simple physical ways of thinking about complex physical-spiritual matters. The role of the rock in the play is to roll away. This is what the boy finally realizes. What he has been doing in each performance is exactly what rocks are supposed to do: roll away so that truth can be seen.

And suddenly—which is how it usually happens—the rock of his own mind rolled away and he glimpsed a world where huge rocks are no big thing.

Roll, Rock, roll!

The Smoker

French spiritual master G. I. Gurdjieff had a directee who came to him and said that she thought she was progressing well in the spiritual life. However, she was addicted to smoking.

Gurdjieff said, "Well, you probably should do something about that."

The woman went away and after a period of about a year she came back and told Gurdjieff that she had, indeed, beaten the addiction. She was no longer a smoker.

Gurdjieff said, "Good."

Then he pulled out a pack of cigarettes and said, "Have a cigarette."

In Nikos Kazantzakis' novel Zorba the Greek, the boss asks Zorba what a man is. Zorba replies with a story about his father. Every day his father would leave the house early in the morning and walk seven miles to begin plowing and planting a field. Before he would begin his day's work, he would sit down under a tree, fill his pipe with tobacco, and have a leisurely smoke. One day when the father opened his tobacco pouch, it was empty. He went into a rage and ripped the tobacco pouch to shreds. Then he stopped and realized what he had done. From that day forward he never smoked again. Zorba ended the tale with, "That is a man."

To be human is to be transcendent—to be a little bit more than our habits and behaviors.

When we become so addicted to our habits that they can reduce us to rage, it is time to assert our independence. We humans are constantly breaking out of the prisons we ourselves have constructed. We play all the roles—warden, guard and inmate. But the moment we most enjoy is when we are dancing in freedom on the far side of the wall.

The story of "The Smoker" takes this freedom a step further. Gurdjieff wants his disciple free of all addictions. This means she does not have to smoke and does not have to not-smoke. She is only truly free if she can take one puff and stop. The master is pushing the ability to eat one potato chip. "Can stop eating 'em" is Gurdjieff's slogan, "and can start eating 'em." A marketing nightmare!

The Hindus have a phrase, "Renounce and enjoy!" It means that we can only enjoy what we are not attached to. Does the drunkard enjoy wine? Does the glutton enjoy food? Do the sexually addicted enjoy sex? Spiritual teachers say "not really." They think our capacity for pleasure is related to our ability to detach ourselves from compulsive behaviors. Spiritual development is not about sacrificing things but about enjoying things. And the way to enjoyment is through the experience of freedom.

"Here, have a cigarette," is not a directive we should explore from the point of view of current medical knowledge. It is a symbolic remark that lights up the path of freedom.

We Are Three,
You Are Three

When the bishop's ship stopped at a remote island for a day, he determined to use the day as profitably as possible. He strolled along the seashore and came across three fishermen mending their nets. In pidgin English they explained to him that centuries before they had been Christianized by missionaries. "We, Christians!" they said, proudly pointing to themselves.

The bishop was impressed. Did they know the Lord's Prayer? They had never heard of it. The bishop was shocked. How could these men claim to be Christians when they did not know something as elementary as the Lord's Prayer?

"What do you say, then, when you pray?" the bishop asked.

"We lift eyes in heaven. We pray, 'We are three, you are three, have mercy on us.' " The bishop was appalled at the primitive, the downright heretical nature of their prayer. So he spent the whole day teaching them to say the Lord's Prayer. The fishermen were poor learners, but they gave it all they had and before the bishop sailed away the next day he had the satisfaction of hearing them go through the whole formula without a fault.

Months later the bishop's ship happened to pass by those islands and the bishop, as he paced the deck saying his evening prayers, recalled with pleasure that fact that on that distant island were three men who were now able to pray correctly, thanks to his patient efforts. While he was lost in thought he happened to look up and noticed a spot of light in the east. The light kept approaching the ship and, as the bishop gazed in wonder, he saw three figures walking on the water towards the boat. The captain stopped the boat and all the sailors leaned over the rails to see this amazing sight.

When they were within speaking distance, the bishop recognized his three friends, the fishermen. "Bishop!"

they exclaimed, "we so glad met you. We hear your boat go past island and come hurry hurry meet you."

"What is it you want?" asked the bishop in awe.

"Bishop," they said, "we so sorry. We forget lovely prayer. We say: 'Our Father in heaven, holy be your name, your kingdom come'...then we forget. Please tell us whole prayer again."

The bishop felt humbled. "Go back to your homes, my good men," he said, "and each time you pray, say, 'We are three, you are three, have mercy on us!'"

I like the bishop in this story. He is self-important, judgmental and pompous. But he knows the real thing when he sees it. I know more than one religious professional who would have arrogantly continued the formal education of the miraculously light-enveloped trio, even after they walked on the water:

"Now let's see. How far did you get? Next is 'Give us this day our daily bread.' Please repeat it."

But this bishop is not so formula-attached that he is dulled to what is happening. His heart is not hardened, and he quickly and sincerely repents. His conversion is signaled by what he says to the fishermen, "Go back to your homes, my good men, and each time you pray, say, 'We are three, you are three, have mercy on us!' " This is the prayer he had previously thought was "downright heretical." What sounded heretical became orthodox when he observed its effects. The story says that the bishop felt humbled. But from another perspective he has been elevated, elevated into the higher truth about prayer.

What is that truth?

The truth is that prayer is not ultimately about words but about communion with God. And when communion with God is evident the words that made the contact—no matter what they were—were ipso facto the right ones.

But there might be an even more subtle truth

hidden in the words, "We are three, you are three." If God is three and they are three, these simple fishermen realize, then they have something in common with the divine life. Their prayer gives them a sense of participation in God, not a sense of distance or unworthiness.

When we come at prayer as creatures—limited, weak, helpless—we pray as creatures for strength from the all-powerful One. When we come at it as sinners, we pray for forgiveness and freedom from the errors, mistakes and failings which imprison us.

But what if we sensed we are children of God, that there is between us and the divine a real link, a bonding unbreakable? Would not our prayer produce in us a lightness, an ability to walk over the waves of danger?

Prayer is the way we meet and open ourselves to the divine, and whatever words make that happen are sacred. The one who said, "Not everyone who says, 'Lord, Lord,' will enter the kingdom of God," knew the limits of prayer formulas. He also knew that people are a blessedness rooted in Blessed-

ness, a light rooted in the Light, a salt rooted in Infinite Zest. When we realize this communion with God, our prayer will no longer be some words we have memorized but— like the three fishermen—the natural overflow of knowing who we are at the deepest level of our selves.

Why Some Trees Are Evergreen

When the plants and trees were first made, the Great Mystery gave a gift to each species. But first he set up a contest to determine which gift would be most useful to whom.

"I want you to stay awake and keep watch over the earth for seven nights," he told them.

The young trees and plants were so excited to be trusted with such an important job that the first night they would have found it difficult *not* to stay awake. However, the second night was not so easy, and just before dawn a few fell asleep. On the third night the trees and plants whispered among themselves in the wind trying to keep from dropping off, but it was too much work for some of them. Even more fell asleep on the fourth night.

By the time the seventh night came the only trees and plants still awake were the cedar, the pine, the spruce, the fir, the holly, and the laurel.

"What wonderful endurance you have!" exclaimed the Great Mystery. "You shall be given the gift of remaining green forever. You will be the guardians of the forest. Even in the seeming dead of winter your brother and sister creatures will find life protected in your branches."

Ever since then all the other trees and plants lose their leaves and sleep all winter, while the evergreens stay awake.

I use this story during the Advent-Christmas season. It ties in with two major themes— wakefulness in the midst of sleepiness, green-

ness in the midst of barrenness. If you add to these two images the images of light in the midst of darkness and love in the midst of rejection, you have the imaginative contrasts that capture the feast of Christmas.

These images unfold a message of strength and defiance. The surrounding world may be asleep or barren or dark or rejecting, but it cannot completely close our eyes, wither our greenness, snuff out our light, or destroy our love. Although we may not reflect on it, there is an edge to Christmas, an in-your-face attitude. Chesterton put it simply and well: "A religion that defies the world should have a feast that defies the weather."

If I ever return to the custom of sending Christmas cards, the cover will be a picture of a light shining in the darkness or a wide-awake person amid sleepers or an evergreen in the midst of a barren forest or a laughing child in a ramshackle stable. Inside, the greeting will be straightforward: "Have a Defiant Christmas!"

Although it is not on the standard list of Christian virtues, I have come to see gentle defiance as a key attitude of the spiritual life. So much in everyone's life and in the life of our society has to be acknowledged and worked with but not given any ultimate status. We do not blind ourselves to what is negative, but neither do we embrace negativities as if they have a right to exist. At one time or another our health is precarious, our work life stressful or imperiled, our finances shaky, our relationships in need of repair, our society splintered, and our culture insane. Yet we give in to none of these forces. We refuse their right to shape us. We defy their efforts at domination. "In the world you will have tribulations, but cheer up. I have overcome the world," Jesus said in the Gospel of John.

It is important that this defiance be gentle. It cannot be angry and raging, finding fuel in hatred. That type of defiance is a bonfire that quickly goes out, its energy rapidly depleted. Gentle defiance comes from our contact with a power of love that is stronger than all the things that try to tear us down and destroy us.

This power of love transcends all there is and yet suffuses all there is. Ultimately, we are bonded to this love beyond all breaking. Our gentle defiance springs from this everlasting relationship. It is not a tirade or a well-crafted act or a compulsive trait of our personality. It is simply who we are—awake among the sleeping, green in the midst of the barren, light shining in the darkness, loving steadily though non-love abounds.

Be gently defiant and "your brother and sister creatures will find life protected in your branches."

The Woman
and the Kid
in Lincoln Park

One Saturday morning I was smoking a cigar in Chicago's Lincoln Park and looking over toward the zoo. Ahead of me, turning onto the far end of the walk, was a young woman about the age of thirty-five and a boy of eight or nine.

They were walking toward me down the walk. Grassy hills sloped up on both sides of them. As I'm watching them while puffing on my cigar, the woman suddenly turns, grabs the boy's hand, and says something to him. I couldn't hear what she said, but whatever it was pushed his button. He took a swing at her—but it was one of those eight-year-old swings that by the time it gets there it has lost everything.

Besides that, the woman ducked under it like a skilled boxer, and as he swung she pulled him against her, his face into her stomach. The boy flailed away at her shoulder blades. Then he tried to kick her. When he tried to kick her he lost his footing and slid down a little bit. But the woman had a tight grip on him and pulled him up. Then she took his hair, pulled his head back, and looked down on him. Even though it was far away, I could see he was crying.

Then she lost her grip. The boy spun away from her and ran up the side of the hill. She began to run after him but, although she was stronger than he was, she was not as fast. He got away from her.

The woman went back to the sidewalk and began to walk again toward me. When the boy got far enough up on the top of the hill, he turned around and yelled, "I don't like you!"

The woman yelled back, "You don't have to like me. You have to listen to me!"

It was only then that I was *sure* she was his mother.

What happened next was like a scene from an old

cowboy movie. The mother was the wagon train down in the valley and the son was the Indians up on the hill. He'd come down the hill and get close to her. She'd go after him and he'd run away. This happened about two or three times—he'd come down and get close, then run away; come down and get close, and then run away.

Finally, he got too close and, in the three fastest steps of her adult life, she tackled him. She threw him down on the ground, sat on his stomach, pinned his arms against the grass with her knees, and then gave him a nuggie on his head!

Exhausted, she rolled off him and lay there on the grass huffing and puffing. (Thirty-five-year-olds can't do a lot without huffing and puffing.)

The boy sat up and just did nothing for a minute. Then suddenly he jumped on her and began to tickle and tickle and tickle and tickle and tickle and tickle her. And she began to laugh and laugh and laugh and laugh and laugh and laugh. Then he began to laugh and laugh and laugh and laugh and laugh and laugh.

Finally there was only the sound of their laughter and the smoke of my cigar rising like incense over Lincoln Park.

A long-lasting relationship is made up of a thousand breaks and a thousand mendings.

Paradoxically, this process of breaking and mending does not make the bond weaker but stronger. The reason is that we can begin to understand our part in how things break and in how things mend. Most of us never get good enough to prevent the breaks, but most of us do get inventive and creative enough to pursue the mending. The key to mending is to think not that you are putting something back together again but that you are creating something completely new out of what broke. It is not a matter of going back. It is a matter of going forward, of integrating events into larger and larger wholes.

As I watched the mother and son in Lincoln Park, I realized she was integrating their break into the larger world of "young boy roughhousing and rassling." Playfulness and laughter was the path she discovered. She bypassed the (sometimes) equally effective paths of scrutiny, explanation, apologies and firm purposes of amendments.

In this case, at least, the serious adult world, with its addiction to words, words, words, would do nothing but bog down the possibilities. The game had already begun. Why not continue it? Hit and break, come close but don't get caught, come too close and get caught, wrestle in a fake fight where every touch is renewed contact, end in laughter that transcends the ruptured world and brings it back into harmony.

To make reconciliation a reality we need multiple images of reconciliation "taking place." Political presidents signing peace treaties while cameras click and bent-over popes in prison cells with their would-be assassins are a start.

But more ordinary coming-togethers also have to capture our imaginations. Handshakes, dinners at round tables, embraces, smiles—even tickling—should become part of our inner cinema that shows us reconciliation is possible. We have to be reminded that the art of living is learning how to create new mosaics out of the fragments of what we ourselves have broken.

We are all called to be artists and—when the situation arises—wrestlers...like the woman and the kid in Lincoln Park.

Sources
of the Stories

The question of the source of a story is often a difficult one. Where I took a story directly from another book, I have given proper credit. Where I have told a story as I heard it or made it up, I have listed my book or audio tape where it can be found. If I learn in the future the original source of a story, I will acknowledge that in further editions of this book.

"The Antique Watch" from *Gospel Spirituality* by John Shea, Side A (ACTA Publications)

"Both Here and There" from *The Path of the Everyday Hero* by Lorna Catford and Michael Ray (Jeremy P. Tarcher, Inc.)

"The Christmas Phone Call" from *The Spirit Master* by John Shea (Thomas More Press)

"The Fasting of the Heart" from *The Way of Chuang Tzu* by Thomas Merton (New Directions Publishing Corporation)

"The Fasting Monk" from *Dynamics of the Spiritual Life* by John Shea, Side K (ACTA Publications)

"The Father's Bowl" from *The Religious Dimension of Family Life* by John Shea, Side A (ACTA Publications)

"God's Fruit Stand" from *The Spiritual Center of Christmas* by John Shea, Side A (ACTA Publications)

"The Grieving Woman and the Spiritual Master" from *Dynamics of the Spiritual Life* by John Shea, Side H (ACTA Publications)

"The Helper and the Homeless Woman" from *How Can I Help?* by Ram Dass and Paul Gorman (Alfred A. Knopf, Inc.)

"The Irritable Man" from *Dynamics of the Spiritual Life* by John Shea, Side A (ACTA Publications)

"The Jumping Mouse" from *Seven Arrows* by Hyemeyohsts Storm (HarperCollins)

"Junk!" from *How Can I Help?* by Ram Dass and Paul Gorman (Alfred A. Knopf, Inc.)

"The Legend of the Bells" from *The Song of the Bird* by Anthony de Mello (Gujarat Sahitya Prakash)

"Lord Krishna and the Two Kings" from *Stories of the Spirit, Stories of the Heart* edited by Christina Feldman and Jack Kornfield (HarperCollins)

"The Man on the Ox" from *Dynamics of the Spiritual Life* by John Shea, Side B (ACTA Publications)

"Nasrudin and the Hot Peppers" from *Dynamics of the Spiritual Life* by John Shea, Side E (ACTA Publications)

"Nasrudin and the Perfect Woman" from *Dynamics of the Spiritual Life* by John Shea, Side A (ACTA Publications)

"The Obedient and the Disobedient Servants" from *Dynamics of the Spiritual Life* by John Shea, Side E (ACTA Publications)

"Paint the Other Side" from *The Spirit Master* by John Shea (Thomas More Press)

"The Prince and the Monkey" from *Dynamics of the Spiritual Life* by John Shea, Side E (ACTA Publications)

"The Rock" from *The Christian in the World* by John Shea, Tape 2, Side B (ACTA Publications)

"The Smoker" from *Dynamics of the Spiritual Life* by John Shea, Side K (ACTA Publications)

"We Are Three, You Are Three" from *The Song of the Bird* by Anthony de Mello (Gujarat Sahitya Prakash)

"Why Some Trees Are Evergreen" from *The Solstice Evergreen* by Sheryl Karas (Aslan Publishing)

"The Woman and the Kid in Lincoln Park" from *The Religious Dimension of Family Life* by John Shea, Side A (ACTA Publications)

Also by John Shea from ACTA Publications

Also by John Shea from ACTA Publications